The Unmasking of 'Ksan

Books by Eric Wilson

The Tom and Liz Austen Mysteries

Also available by Eric Wilson

The Unmasking of 'Ksan

by

ERIC WILSON

HarperCollins*Publishers*Ltd

As in his other mysteries, Eric Wilson writes here about imaginary people in a real landscape.

Find Eric Wilson at http://hypbus.com/ewilson/

http://www. harpercollins.com

First published in hardcover by Collins Publishers: 1986
First published in paperback by Collins Publishers: 1987
First HarperCollins Publishers Ltd paperback edition: 1990
    Third printing: 1994
Revised paperback edition published by HarperCollins Publishers Ltd: 1996
    Second printing: 1998

Canadian Cataloguing in Publication Data

Wilson, Eric
   The unmasking of 'Ksan

ISBN 0-00-648187-6

I. Title.

PS8595.I583U5 1996   jC813'.54   C95-933357-6
PZ7.W55Un 1996

---

   00 01 02 03 04 OPM 10 9 8 7 6 5 4 3

Printed and bound in the United States

cover design: Richard Bingham
cover and chapter illustrations: Richard Row
logo photograph: Lawrence McLagan

Dedicated to the Gitksan

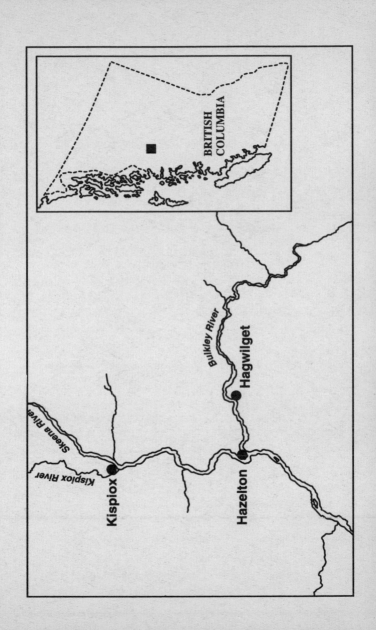

1

GrrrrrrrrROAR!

The terrible sound came from Bear, crouched in the doorway. Firelight glowed in his fur and flickered against his mask.

Snarling, Bear moved toward me.

I tried to look brave as he came close, growling low in his throat.

Suddenly, his paw lashed out.

I flinched as the long claws glittered in the firelight. Then Bear's head tilted and the mask's blank eyes stared into mine. Nearby people laughed, then looked nervous as Bear moved on, searching for another victim.

Two Native boys used poles to herd Bear past the fire burning in the middle of the communal house.

Several teenage girls sat near the fire, showing no fear as Bear approached. Then one girl stood up. Tangling her fingers into Bear's fur, she quickly wrestled him to the ground.

Released by the girl, Bear retreated. Still snarling, still taking swipes at the audience, he was driven by the boys toward the door. As he disappeared into the night I could hear sighs of relief around me. Even though Bear was just part of the performance, the mask and claws made him seem awfully real.

A man with a camera sat beside me. "What a great show. Where are you from?"

"Right here in Hazelton. I've come to watch my friend Dawn. She's one of the dancers."

"This is my first trip to northern British Columbia. I wouldn't have missed these dancers for anything."

Other tourists sat around us on wooden benches. Nearby was the fire, blazing in the middle of the dirt floor. Steps led to the stage where the dancers performed. Above it was the painted crest of the Wolf Clan, and to each side stood thick totem poles supporting the roof beams. As the fire's smell drifted toward me, I watched a dancer wearing a sun mask come on stage. Drums sounded as forest creatures entered to dance, followed by loons in blue robes and delicately carved masks.

"What do these dances mean, anyway?"

"I'm not sure," I replied. "Dawn told me they're thousands of years old and . . ."

"You mean we're watching dances that have been performed that long? Amazing!"

"I know they tell the legends of the Gitksan people.

Those loons were making fun of a clumsy chief who fell into a lake."

"What about the bear? It sure was dramatic."

"That dance represents some kind of spirit power of the chiefs. I don't know what it means, exactly. Only the Gitksan know the secret meaning of their dances."

"Tell me something," the tourist said. "They call this place 'Ksan, but what's it for? When I parked my car and walked in past the totem poles I saw all these big wooden houses in a row. What's inside the other ones?"

"A couple show how the Natives used to live before Europeans arrived. In one of them you can watch totems and masks being made by carvers."

"So it's kind of a living museum. How do you pronounce the name?"

"The k is hard, like in the word kid."

"So it's k-san." The man smiled. "This is a beautiful area in the summer, but I bet there's lots of snow the rest of the year. Do you go to school here in Hazelton?"

I nodded. "I'm in grade nine. So's Dawn."

"So where is this friend of yours? Have we seen her dance yet?"

I shook my head. "You'll know when Dawn's on stage. She's sensational, good enough to go professional. Her raven dance is next." I leaned closer so I could whisper. "Don't tell anyone, but this is a very special performance for her."

"Why's that?"

"Dawn's going to dance in a mask she borrowed from the 'Ksan museum this evening. It's incredibly old and priceless."

"Is that so? Doesn't she usually dance with a mask, then?"

"Yes, but she uses an imitation mask carved by her brother."

"So why bother using the old one, if it's so valuable?"

I shrugged. "Something about feeling close to her ancestors. She tried to explain it to me, but it didn't mean much." Voices chanted off-stage, followed by the beat of a drum. "Here she comes now."

As the drum grew louder Dawn appeared in a robe of black feathers. Her face was completely hidden by the magnificent raven mask with its powerful beak. Firelight shone on the red and black designs as she spread her arms like wings and began to dance. Her feet hardly seemed to touch the stage as she moved faster and faster, while the chanting and drum beat grew louder. Around me the tourists leaned forward, captured by the pounding drum and the swift motion of Dawn's feet and arms as she whirled around and around the stage, becoming a blur of energy.

Suddenly, the dance ended and she stood motionless. With a swift movement, the raven's beak opened to reveal another mask inside—the staring face of a human. As the audience gasped in surprise, and the human mask shone in the firelight, the door behind us crashed open.

Bear had returned.

Although a few people glanced his way, most were still swept up in the drama of Dawn's performance. But I was confused. Never before had Bear appeared twice in the same performance. The young dancers backstage must have been puzzled, too, because faces appeared around the wings of the stage. Then someone shouted in astonishment.

Bear was holding a revolver.

He ran swiftly across the dirt floor, leapt onto the stage and pointed the revolver at Dawn. Some of the tourists were grinning, thinking this was part of the act, but the dancers were horrified. A couple of them moved to protect Dawn, then froze when Bear waved the revolver in their direction.

Dawn seemed to understand what Bear wanted. With shaking hands she took off the raven mask and handed it to him. He jumped down from the stage and headed for the door. It all happened so quickly that no one even tried to stop him.

Then he was gone into the night. Some tourists leapt up, shouting for help, while others grabbed their children to stop them from crying. The kids on stage were also making a racket, so the noise was unbelievable. Finally it was stopped by a woman who appeared from backstage and raised both hands, calling for quiet.

"Please calm down. You're not in any danger."

"Oh, yeah?" shouted a man. "That thing, that . . . creature . . . might come back! I'm getting out of here."

"You're free to leave. The rest of the performance is cancelled."

"Aren't you going to phone the police?"

"Of course. But at night there are only a couple of officers on duty, and they're often far from Hazelton patrolling the highway. It may take a while for help to get here."

The man beside me looked at her. "Are you in charge here?"

"Yes. My name is Grace Heslin. I'm the dance director."

"Do you know what's going on? What's this all about?"

Grace turned to look at Dawn, still standing at the front of the stage. Her long black hair was a mess from being jammed inside the mask, and make-up was smudged around her dark eyes. She was trembling, and I could tell that she was trying hard not to cry.

"I made a mistake. It was . . ." Dawn swallowed, then shook her head. Running a hand through her hair, she glanced at the other dancers and then turned to the tourists. "I wanted to dance with the raven mask that has been in my family for many generations. I wanted to feel the strength of my forefathers as I danced in their mask. Today I went to the museum, then . . ."

"Then," Grace interrupted, "you took the mask despite being warned not to."

A woman in the audience stood up. "I don't understand. Why was the mask stolen?"

"It's worth a fortune," Grace explained. "That mask is very, very old. It's a unique treasure of the Gitksan people, so it would be very valuable to a collector. Most of them won't touch stolen artifacts, but there are some crooked collectors who would pay a huge amount of money to get that raven mask."

"Why did the museum let this girl use the mask?"

"It belongs to her family. She had the right to use it."

"And her parents approved?"

Grace looked at Dawn, who was staring numbly at the dying fire. "Her parents are out of town," she sighed. "They're dancers, too, and right now they're in Idaho with the other adults. That's why the teenagers and children are on stage this evening. I'm sure Dawn chose this time to borrow the mask because her parents couldn't say no."

One of the tourists looked at Dawn. "I must say, you sure handed over the mask in a hurry."

"I was scared! There was a gun in my face."

"It could have been a fake. Besides, how did you know he wanted the mask?"

"What else was he after? My autograph? Everyone in town knew I was borrowing the mask from the museum tonight. People even stopped me in the street to say how irresponsible I was."

"And you still wouldn't listen? You took a priceless mask out of safe-keeping and had it ready to hand over when that guy came running in with a gun?"

"Are you saying that I'd steal from my own people?"

The man just shrugged.

"Well, mister, let me tell you something." Dawn's black eyes cut into the man. She was really angry, and she looked wonderful. "You can take back every word because the mask is safe."

"What?"

As Grace frowned, Dawn left the stage. Voices murmured, followed by cries of surprise as she returned. In her hands was the raven mask. I laughed out loud, but I was confused. What was going on?

"You see?" Dawn held up the mask. "It's perfectly safe."

The tourist's mouth was hanging open. "But . . . how. . .?"

"This evening, before I went on stage, I got dressed in the raven regalia. But I couldn't put on the mask. Somehow it seemed wrong. So I hid it backstage, and wore the modern copy instead."

"So the person with the gun stole the copy?"

"Yes. I'm holding the original mask."

Some of the tourists applauded, and others laughed at the man who'd given Dawn a rough time. Then they headed for the door. But Grace didn't look amused, and I couldn't tell what the other dancers were thinking as they went backstage to change. Dawn went, too, and I hung around the fire because I'd arranged to walk home with her.

"Can you get the mask back into the museum tonight?" I asked Grace.

"Let's hope so. Josh has gone to Ray West's house. He's the curator in charge of the museum, so he'll be able to unlock it and put the mask back." She poked angrily at the dying fire with a stick. The embers flared, lighting up her face. "Kids these days are so irresponsible."

"Hey, that's not fair. Can you blame Dawn for wanting to dance in that old mask so much?"

"No, but it was pretty sneaky of her to wait for her parents to leave town. They'd never have given her permission to borrow the mask from the museum. That thing is priceless. When I think of it being stolen I break out in a cold sweat."

Then Dawn appeared with the raven mask. Right away I felt better, just seeing her face.

"Wow, what an evening," I said to her. "It gave me a bunch of ideas for my film. Dawn, you've got to star in it. The whole thing would centre around this innocent girl, see, who gets attacked by a . . ."

She ran a hand through her long hair. "Graham, let's not talk movies tonight, okay? I'm not up to it."

"But what's the matter? You faked the crook out of the mask, and you sure fixed that tourist. Did he ever look sick when you brought out the real mask!"

Dawn gave me a faint smile, then turned to Grace. "I'm really sorry I took it out of the museum. When Bear jumped onto the stage with the gun, I thought . . ."

I looked at her suddenly. "Hey, I wonder why he didn't notice you were wearing the copy?"

"The light's so dim in here, I guess he couldn't tell. Besides, Ezra's copy looks just like the original."

"Who do you think the thief was?"

Dawn shook her head. "Definitely not Hal. He made the first appearance as Bear, being herded with the poles, but he went backstage after that. When I started my dance I saw Hal watching from the wings. He was still wearing the regalia and holding his bear mask."

"That means the guy with the gun somehow got his hands on a bearskin and a mask. There can't be many of those around. I'll bet the police will find their man in no time."

Dawn glanced at me. "Lots of bear masks have been made by Ezra and the other 'Ksan carvers, and every second house in Hazelton has a bearskin on the wall."

"So, no problem." I grinned. "Those bearskins are

all dusty with age. The police just raid every house, find the bearskin that's had a good airing tonight, and arrest the owner. *Voilà!* The case is solved."

"Sherlock Holmes to the rescue, eh? What if the crook used a bearskin from a house in Moricetown or Telkwa?"

"Come on, Dawn, relax. I'm just trying to make you feel better. The mask is safe."

Grace nodded. "Let's save the jokes until the mask is back in the museum."

I picked up the mask and studied the old wood. Those things didn't usually mean much to me, but I couldn't help feeling impressed. I mean, imagine some young guy sitting by a mountain stream centuries ago, carving this thing. Now here I was, holding it in my own hands.

"I'm sorry I don't know more about your culture, but what does this mask mean? Why does the raven's beak open to show a human face inside?"

"We believe that animals, humans and spirits are one and the same. Sometimes spirits come down from the heavens in the shape of birds, then turn into humans." Grace tugged on some strings, opening the beak to show the staring wooden face inside. "Here you see the raven transformed into a man."

"You mean I could be the brother of a mountain goat?"

She smiled. "Sure, or the brother of a beetle burrowed deep inside a log in the forest. That's why we respect all nature, because we're one with it and take our strength from it."

I looked around the communal house, wishing I

knew more about Gitksan customs. When we moved to Hazelton my mom started right in to learn everything, talking to people and reading books, but I was too wrapped up with computers to make the same effort. Then it was too late to ask her questions.

"Where on earth is Ray?" Grace held her watch close to the fire, trying to read the time. "He just lives up the hill. Why isn't he here yet?"

"Maybe Josh couldn't find him," Dawn suggested.

"I'd better check. You two wait here, and keep an eye on that mask."

"Don't worry, Grace. Nothing will happen to it now."

"I won't rest until it's locked safely inside the museum, like it always should have been."

After Grace was gone, Dawn and I sat silently, staring at the embers as the smoke drifted toward the ceiling. Through the smoke-hole, I could see the last colours of a sunset. Soon the night would be as black as the inside of the communal house. I looked at the darkly shadowed totems supporting the roof beams, wondering if I could film in these tricky lighting conditions. Then I turned to Dawn.

"You're sure quiet."

"It's been a rough evening."

As she stared at the embers I studied her huge dark eyes and beautiful mouth. Suddenly I felt a little nervous. I wished I had the courage to move a little closer to her. But I knew I would probably be wasting my time. Dawn just thought of me as a friend, a buddy. And I couldn't figure out how to get her to change her mind.

So I stayed where I was, watching the glowing light of the embers on her face and hair. Then the door opened and I turned to see if Grace had returned with Ray West, the curator.

But it wasn't them in the doorway. It was Bear.

2

Fear rose inside me as I stared at the creature. I wanted to run but I was frozen. The mask was so frightening with its snarling mouth and empty, staring eyes.

Dawn sprang toward the fire. Swiftly she scooped dirt from the floor over the embers. Suddenly the communal house was in darkness, touched only by faint light seeping through the smoke-hole above.

A hand slipped into mine. "Come on," Dawn whispered, pulling me up from the bench. On shaking legs I stumbled after her through the darkness, then tripped and fell to my knees. I crawled forward until my head smashed against something hard. I yelped in pain, then felt Dawn's hand cover my mouth.

My eyes searched the darkness for Bear. The narrow door was open, showing the nearby forest, but there was no sign of the creature. "Get ready to run," Dawn whispered. She put her hand in mine and I could sense her body tensing. Then with sudden force she pulled me toward the door. Somehow I managed to scramble to my feet and raced with her in the direction of the light. Inside my head a voice screamed *don't shoot!* and then we burst out of the communal house. Directly above us was a totem pole showing the huge eyes and teeth of Wolf. Gasping for air, I raced with Dawn toward the shelter of the forest.

"He's coming after us!"

Looking back, I saw Bear near the doorway. I knew he'd never stop chasing us while Dawn had the raven mask.

"Get rid of that thing!"

"Not a chance," she said. "Come on, run faster!"

There was no point arguing. Still expecting to feel a bullet crash into my body, I threw myself toward the forest. It seemed we'd never reach it, then suddenly the trees were all around. I sucked air into my burning lungs, then followed Dawn as she pushed past heavy ferns and low bushes.

"I know a hiding place," she said. "Keep moving, Graham. That guy can't run fast in a heavy bearskin."

At last we neared the river and crawled inside a hollow log. I put my head against the spongy wood and gasped for air, but Dawn wasn't even breathing hard. Instead she put a finger to her lips, then listened intently. I could hear the river rushing past, and the harsh cries of the ravens in the trees, but nothing else.

At long last Dawn leaned close. "I think we're safe."

"This is crazy! Why did you ever take that mask?"

"It was important to me! Even my brother said I should dance with it. He's the one who suggested getting it from the museum. Imagine, this mask was used by the grandfather of my grandfather."

"This whole thing will make a great sequence for my film."

"I thought you were going to make a horror movie about werewolves stalking their victims through Hazelton or something like that."

"After what happened tonight I'm thinking of calling it *The Attack of the Killer Bear*. Can't you see the opening credits? There's a close-up of the mask's glistening fangs. Then the camera pans slowly back, revealing those gross nostrils and the staring eyes. Already the faint-hearted will be screaming for the exits."

"Don't you want them to stay for the rest of your movie?"

"No way! People screaming into the streets is solid-gold publicity." I tapped my head. "This little item is always thinking, Dawn. Always thinking."

She laughed and shook her head. "You don't quit, do you? For a minute you even made me forget that guy and his gun."

"What's going to happen now?"

She paused to think. "We don't know where the curator is, or Grace. Until the museum can be unlocked we need to hide the mask." She wriggled out of hiding. "Come on, I know a good place."

She led the way through the forest, finding a trail where I saw nothing but a black wall of trees and

bushes. A few minutes later we paused at the edge of
the forest, looking at the spotlights shining above
'Ksan. The totem poles were deeply shadowed, but the
glow from one spotlight showed the teeth and eyes of
Wolf outside the communal house where all this trouble had begun.

My eyes searched for Bear, then I looked up at the
shapes of dark clouds moving across the night sky. The
air was clean and somewhere a bird called. I shivered.

Dawn touched my arm. "Let's hide the mask first,
then come back here to find out what's happened to
Ray and Grace."

Staying close to the trees, we moved cautiously
around the edge of 'Ksan and then climbed a road that
led to some of Hazelton's houses. The town is actually
built on a series of "benches" of land, so some streets
are down by the river, others are up higher, while the
only thing on the highest bench is the graveyard.

Lights shone from the windows of some houses we
passed. I guess in the old days there'd have been totem
poles in front of the Natives' homes, but now you only
saw cars and pickups. As Dawn opened her door she
called her brother's name but there was no answer.

"Ezra must be out. I was really hoping to ask him
what to do."

Dawn went down the hallway to her bedroom.
Opening the cupboard, she pushed a bunch of shoes
aside and lifted a large piece of wood away from the
wall. Inside a dark space I saw the dull gleam of copper pipes.

"The bathroom's on the other side of this crawl
space. The only time this is opened is when the

plumber works on the pipes. It's a perfect place to hide the mask." Carefully she rested the mask against the copper pipes, then put the wood back into place and straightened the shoes.

"I wish your parents weren't in Idaho. They'd know what to do."

"Are you kidding? I'm glad they're in Idaho. By the time they get home all the excitement will have died down. Maybe I won't even get grounded for a year."

I grinned. "You deserve to be grounded for years. I've had fourteen heart attacks tonight." As we returned to the living room I looked at the Native prints on the wall near the TV set. They were beautiful, but even better were the masks that Ezra had carved showing Bear, Eagle and Man-with-Frog-in-Mouth. One that really freaked me was the Ghost mask. It was like a skull, with a white face and staring eyes, and it showed moss growing over one corner of the mouth. Every time I visited Dawn's house I stared at that mask, trying to decide on the best way to use it in my film.

"Come on, Graham, let's get moving."

The air outside was warm and a yellow moon had appeared over the huge mountain that rises above Hazelton. Maps call it Rocher du Boule, but Mom always used the Native name of Stek'yaw'den.

Approaching along the road was a guy named Connor Gentry. He was a 'Ksan artist, famous for his totem poles and sarcastic comments. Dawn moved closer to me and her voice dropped. "Don't tell Connor what happened."

But it was clear he'd already heard. He grabbed

Dawn's arm as we tried to pass. The cheeks of his face were hollow. "That was a pretty stupid thing to do, Dawn. Everyone warned you."

She was silent.

"Where's the real mask now?" His voice was low and angry. I wanted to say something, but could only stare at Connor's silver earring and the glowing cigarette that hung from his mouth.

"I asked you a question! Where's that mask?"

But Dawn just stepped past him.

"Come on, Graham."

"Who does he think he is, bossing you around like that," I whispered as I hurried after her, feeling Connor's eyes boring into my back.

"Connor's okay."

"How can you say that? The guy's always after you, and he's twenty-three years old. Talk about robbing the cradle."

"I haven't gone out with him."

"So what? The jerk keeps right on trying. He should stick to women his own age, but they're probably afraid of getting nicotine poisoning when he breathes on them."

A few minutes later we entered the grounds of 'Ksan. It was in complete darkness except for the glow from a few spotlights. I squinted, trying to force my eyes to penetrate the gloom, then jumped when I heard a loud cry from the forest.

"What was that?"

"Just an animal."

"There's no sign of Grace. Let's get out of here."

Dawn didn't reply. She moved to the wall of the

nearest building, then cautiously worked her way forward. The totem poles ignored her, staring through the night toward the sound of the rushing river.

Then Dawn turned to me. "Somebody just walked past a spotlight over at the museum."

"Was it Grace?"

"I don't think so, but I couldn't tell for sure. We'd better find out."

"Okay, but let's be careful."

We moved quickly to the museum, which stood next to the other buildings. Spotlights on the wall showed crests of the sun and two creatures that looked like birds. As we approached I heard the low murmur of voices, and then two figures emerged from the darkness into the spotlight's glare. I recognized them immediately. They were a Native couple who lived on a big spread of land out on the Kispiox Road and were rumoured to be some kind of bizarre geniuses. Everyone called them the Einsteins, after the guy who discovered atomic energy. Why were they snooping around the museum?

The couple approached the museum door and leaned over the lock, talking quietly to each other. For a moment Dawn watched from her hiding place, then hurried forward.

"What are you doing?" she demanded.

Looking surprised, Pa Einstein turned toward her. "It's Dawn. People say you've become a fine dancer."

"Thank you," she replied. "But why are you here so late?"

Ma Einstein moved closer. In the spotlight's harsh glow her face looked heavily lined. It was long and narrow, and there was a lot of white in her hair, which was pulled back in a ponytail.

"Dawn, we're so upset about the mask. Your parents will be furious to learn it's been lost."

"But didn't you hear? The real mask is safe. I've hidden it until it can be returned to the museum."

"But . . . but people are saying it was stolen. Someone dressed in the Bear regalia took it from you at gunpoint."

"The robber got only a copy. The original is safe."

"That's . . . such a surprise. I'm so pleased."

"How did you know about the robbery?"

"Word travels fast. Everyone knew you'd be dancing with the mask, so naturally the robbery was big news."

"But what are you doing here? The museum closed hours ago."

Pa Einstein smiled. "We've been hired to install a new computer-alarm system for the museum. We were just driving past and decided to check on the nighttime security. We're going to recommend the installation of spotlights at the back of the building."

I looked at him. "Why would someone break into the museum? Why not rob a bank or something?"

"Some artifacts in this place are worth a fortune. A good example is the raven mask that someone almost managed to steal from Dawn." He pointed to some marks in the wooden door. "You see that? Earlier this week someone tried to force this door open. That's why we've been hired to install the alarm."

I looked at Dawn. "Maybe it was the same person who tried to steal your mask."

She nodded. "Why can't people just leave our treasures alone?"

Ma Einstein looked at her. "Where is the real mask now?"

"Up at my house. There's a crawl space where I've . . ."

Loud voices interrupted Dawn. We all turned toward the darkness, squinting to see against the spotlight's glare. Grace appeared, along with Ray West, the museum curator. Quickly Dawn told them what had happened, then Grace looked at Ray.

"Another delay. I'm sorry, especially after dragging you away from that party."

"No problem. While you're getting the mask I can discuss security ideas with the Einsteins and . . ." He paused, puzzled. "Where have the Einsteins gone?"

I motioned in the direction of the parking lot. "They just walked away. I guess they're going home."

"I can hear the car leaving." Grace beckoned to Dawn. "Let's walk up the hill to your place."

Ray offered me a ride and I jumped at it, because I'd never been inside his car. Long, lean and mean, it had every option money could buy. I'd already decided it was the exact car I'd buy in Hollywood, but this was my first chance to actually ride inside. I'd barely begun to ask questions about it when we reached Dawn's house.

"What a machine!" I grinned at Dawn as I stepped out of the car. "Come with me to L.A. and we'll cruise the streets together. I'll make all your dreams come true."

Grace shook her head at Ray and sighed. "You really shouldn't encourage Graham's dreams of luxury."

He laughed. "Why not? Someone once said that life's nasty, brutish and short, so why not live it in the fast lane?"

"I don't agree, but let's not argue about it now." She turned toward the house. "I just want to get that mask." She opened the door and we followed her inside. The place was dark and silent. As Dawn switched on a lamp I felt goosebumps rise on my skin, and somehow I knew that things had gone terribly wrong. I followed in silence as Grace led the way to Dawn's bedroom. As she knelt down to lift away the wooden covering from the crawl space, I wondered how she knew exactly where the mask was hidden, then realized Dawn must have told her while they were walking up the hill.

"It's not here." Grace looked at Dawn. "You must have put it somewhere else."

Dawn dropped to her knees and stared at the empty space. The copper pipes gleamed in the light, but there was no sign of the mask. She looked at me with horrified eyes. "Graham, the mask is gone."

I just nodded, wishing I could think of something to say. "Maybe . . . maybe Ezra came home and got it."

Grace stared at the two of us. "Is this some kind of game? Where's the mask?"

Dawn ran a hand through her hair. "It was right here. We left it here no more than an hour ago. Graham, how could it be gone?"

I shrugged, feeling helpless. There were tears in Dawn's eyes, and she hugged her body as she stared at the empty crawl space.

"I wish Ezra was here," she said. "He'd know what to do."

At that moment we heard the front door open. Ray West smiled. "Well, speak of the devil. Here's Ezra now."

I looked over his shoulder and saw Dawn's brother at the far end of the hallway. The lamplight shone on his black hair and lit the strong features of his face. I sighed in relief. Ezra would clean up this mess in a hurry. He walked slowly toward us, staring at all the people crowded into his house in the middle of the night.

"What's going on?"

Everyone started talking at once. Ezra tried to follow our babbling, then waved us into the living-room. After we sat down, Dawn told him what had happened, then suddenly burst into tears. As Ezra put an arm around her, I glanced at Grace and Ray. They were leaning back in their chairs, watching Dawn with narrowed eyes. Suddenly my temper flared.

"Dawn didn't steal the mask! She made an honest mistake, and now you're blaming her for it. So what if it's gone? Ezra can carve another one, and make it twice as fancy as that old thing."

Grace glanced at me. "It's sweet of you to stick up for your friend, Graham, but you're not a Native so you can't understand what the mask means to us."

"I'm a Native," Ezra said abruptly, "and I have to agree with Graham. The mask can be replaced, so let's not overreact to all this. I'll carve another one for the museum. I know the original mask is important, but it's not a matter of life and death."

Ezra's words made me feel better, but they didn't seem to help Dawn. She kept right on crying, and I could see that her misery was getting to Ezra. His eyes were sad as he hugged his sister, and even Grace seemed to soften. Crossing the room, she touched Dawn's hair.

"Come on, girl," she said gently. "Like Ezra says, it's not a matter of life and death."

This unexpected sympathy only produced more sobs. "It's all my fault! I should never have borrowed the mask. What'll I do if it's gone forever?"

"People will forget," Ezra said. "Give them time."

"What about our folks? They'll hit the roof when they hear about this."

"Let me handle them. I'll think of something to say."

"But, Ezra, there's nothing you can say. The mask is gone, and all because of me. I'll have to live with this mistake for the rest of my life."

"Hey," I said, "the mask isn't necessarily gone forever. Maybe it'll be found." As I looked at Dawn's beautiful face the thought ran through my mind that maybe I could find the mask. That sure would make me special in her eyes. As I ran a mental video of a grateful Dawn throwing her arms around me, there was a knock on the door. Ray opened it, and suddenly the living-room seemed incredibly crowded as two Mounties walked in, along with Connor Gentry.

The 'Ksan carver made himself right at home, sprawling in a chair and immediately lighting a cigarette. "I saw the cop car pull up, and figured I'd find out for myself what's going on."

The Mounties produced notebooks and began asking questions. Most were directed at Dawn, but I added a few details and felt kind of proud as I watched my words being recorded. But then one of the officers said to Dawn, "Were you part of the robbery?"

"Hey!" I shouted. "What is this? Of course Dawn didn't steal the mask. Why are you picking on her this way?"

The Mountie turned to me. "Listen, don't think we suspect your friend, but we have to do our job." She gestured toward the window. "See that bunch of people standing out in the road? As we got out of the car, one of them told me that Dawn helped steal the mask."

Ezra sighed. "How can they be so dumb?"

I looked at him. "It's because of that crazy tourist. He's the one who claimed Dawn was involved in the robbery, and the other dancers heard him."

"That's too bad. Once a rumour like that gets started, it's hard to stop."

"Well," Connor said, "you know what they say. Where there's smoke, there's fire."

Ezra turned to him. "I don't appreciate your sarcasm. You know perfectly well that Dawn's not involved in the theft. You aren't helping, so please go home."

Connor just shrugged and stubbed out his cigarette. Then he left the house without a word. Ezra turned to the Mounties.

"Got any theories?"

"A mask that size isn't easy to hide. Maybe someone was watching as the two kids arrived here with the mask, then left the house a few minutes later without it. Even an amateur burglar would think to try the crawl space for a mask that big." He smiled. "I wish you Hazelton people would lock your doors. We've warned you enough times."

"So," I said, "do you think the thief was a local?"

"Could be," the man replied. "We'll certainly conduct an extensive search, and that may produce results."

I grinned at Dawn. "You see? They'll have the mask back in no time."

"Let's hope so," Ray said. "That raven was my museum's most famous exhibit. A lot of people have come to 'Ksan just to see it."

"And my dancers," Grace protested. "They're famous, too."

The curator laughed. "Don't start our favourite argument again, kiddo." He stood up. "It's pretty late. Let's get going."

As the door closed behind them I turned to the Mounties. "I just remembered something. You know the couple that people call the Einsteins? We met them at 'Ksan and mentioned the mask was hidden in the crawl space. They had time to come up here and steal it."

One of the officers made a note. "We'll check it out, but somehow I can't see the Einsteins being involved. They're respected elders of Dawn's clan. Why steal a mask from their own people?"

I shrugged. "Maybe they need money."

The Mountie turned to Dawn. "We'll do everything possible. If the mask was stolen by someone from Hazelton, it'll take that person a while to locate a crooked dealer willing to buy it. That will give us extra time to investigate."

Ezra shook their hands. "Thanks for your help. We appreciate it."

As soon as the officers had left, Dawn turned to her brother. "Please don't phone our parents."

"They've got to know eventually."

"Sure, but let's wait until they get home. Maybe by then the mask will be found."

Ezra shook his head. "I don't know. They'd want us to phone right away."

"Please, Ezra!"

"Okay, I guess it's the least I can do. I hate to see you so upset. I never should have suggested that you borrow the mask."

I said goodnight and went outside. A few people still stood around in the darkness, staring at the house. I glanced at them, then started home with two goals in my mind.

First, I would make some notes on the night's events. Second, I would figure out a way to find the mask.

3

The next morning I sat on the steps outside my dad's church.

The sun was hot. It reflected from the white walls of the church's bell tower and sparkled against the waters of the Skeena River flowing past. On the far bank of the river the forest surrounded an abandoned cabin that leaned crookedly, its walls black with age.

I opened a package of Smokehouse Almonds and gobbled a few, then fed a handful to my collie, King. I wish I could say he wagged his tail in gratitude, but he doesn't have one. He lost it after being hit by a car. King has weird tastes in food, preferring almonds and waffles to the stuff that comes out of a can. I'd say he's probably my best friend. His fur sure soaked up a lot of my tears when Mom died of cancer last winter.

I gave him the last of the almonds and then licked the inside of the package. I get the almonds from the local Hudson's Bay Company store, a place so old it goes back to the gold rush days. Hazelton has all these great frontier buildings with false fronts and wide verandahs, and the library is actually shaped like one of the old paddlewheelers that brought in the pioneers. As you look at it beside the river you'd swear it's about to chug away downstream, except the windows are full of books and there's no captain inside, just the friendly librarian.

But I think the best thing about Hazelton is Stek'yaw'den, the enormous mountain that rules this town. It's so high that evergreens grow only halfway up its slopes. Above that there's nothing but wide shoulders of bare rock, seamed by crevices full of snow that never melts. Every day the mountain's beauty changes —green, blue, smoky, then wrapped in clouds.

Forming my hands into the shape of a camera lens, I turned around and studied the church for a good angle. I figured the bell tower was a natural for my film. I could just see a night scene with lightning rippling across the sky and rain glistening from the church walls as a human bat suddenly appeared. Wings flapping in the wind, he would crawl slowly down the tower. Lower and lower, and then . . .

I panned directly into my dad's red hair and beard. He'd come silently out of the church and stood on the steps, smiling. "Getting ready to shoot your werewolf movie, son?" He sat down, rubbed King's head, then looked at the sparkling river. "It's a shame about the mask. I've just been praying for its safe return."

I wasn't surprised. Dad prays about everything. He's never missed a day of kneeling at the altar and covering every subject: war, poverty, car accidents, the high cost of food. I know because he prays out loud and I've listened. His favourite line is *Trust in the Lord*, and I know he believes that absolutely.

"Dad, I'm worried about Dawn. She's really upset about the whole thing. She thinks it's all her fault. I've been thinking . . . maybe I could help."

"By doing what?"

"Well, I thought maybe I could try to find the mask."

"Better leave that to the Mounties."

"But I'd sure like to do something for Dawn."

"Why don't you take her to the Kispiox rodeo? It's today, and the weather's perfect."

"Great idea. Maybe I'll go see if she's home."

"Ezra must also be feeling badly. If your mother was still alive I know she'd be upset for them. She was very close to that family." He stood up. "Tell them I'll drop by later. Or maybe I'll see them at the rodeo."

"You'll be out there? Hey, that's terrific."

"I should warn you I'll be with someone."

"Virginia, I suppose." I shook my head. "You're making a big mistake, Dad. You can do better than her."

He squeezed my shoulder with a strong hand. "I know what I'm doing, Graham."

"I'll make you a deal. You dump Virginia and I'll promise her a starring role in my first film. Even Dracula must have had a mother."

"That's not nice, son. I want you to apologize."

"Why?"

"For your rudeness, and for condemning Virginia without making any effort to know her. She's a fine person."

"You're wrong! She's just looking for a husband, and you're the target."

"Graham, Virginia's not looking for marriage and neither am I. Her career is too important to her. As an anthropologist she studies the way different peoples have lived over the centuries, and she has to travel a lot. We enjoy each other's company and that's it. Do you understand, or do I have to repeat everything in words of one syllable?"

"Now you're the one who's being rude."

"You're right, I'm sorry." Dad put his hands on my shoulders. "I know how much you miss your mother, and so do I. But please understand that I get lonely, and it's good to have Virginia to share my feelings with." When I didn't say anything he squeezed my arm gently. "Come on, cheer up. Go and get Dawn, and enjoy the rodeo."

So I hurried home for my camera and then walked through Old Town—which is what locals call the part of Hazelton with the pioneer buildings—to Dawn's house.

She looked terrible. Her eyes were puffy, from crying or lack of sleep, and she hadn't even combed her hair. The living-room curtains were closed, and she was just lying around on the sofa listening to her Walkman. Her T-shirt was so creased it looked like she'd slept in it, and her jeans weren't in much better shape.

She didn't want to see the rodeo. Ezra had already invited her and she'd turned him down. "I'm not into rodeos."

"You were last year. I remember you cheering your head off. A few days later, I asked you to star in my film. That's when we became friends. Hey, if it weren't for rodeos, you would never have met a future famous director!"

"I know." She tried to smile. "But I've had it with rodeos."

"You mean you've had it with people. You're really letting this mask business get to you."

"Sure, and why not? Want to know what happened this morning? I actually had an anonymous phone call, the kind of thing you read about in books."

"What are you talking about?"

"Someone called and accused me of stealing the mask. When I tried to defend myself they hung up."

"Did you recognize the voice?"

"No. Besides, what difference would it make? Everyone hates me."

"What garbage. You sound like a soap opera."

"But it's true, Graham!"

"Don't let a few creeps grind you down. Hiding in your house just shows them they've beaten you. Come on, let's go to Kispiox. It's a fabulous day." I grabbed the curtains and pulled them open. "Look at that sun! Look at that blue sky! I pulled a lot of strings to arrange such perfect weather for you."

Dawn laughed. "You're crazy."

"After the rodeo we'll pig out on shakes. I tell you, this is too good a day to miss."

"Maybe you're right." She got up from the sofa. "You're a good friend."

"So you keep telling me," I muttered, but Dawn just ignored me. She looked at the clock. "We've still got time to meet Ezra. He'll be driving past up the hill and he promised to watch for me."

"Everything's going to be fine."

"I wish I believed that. But come on, let's go have a few laughs."

* * *

Soon we reached the hill overlooking Old Town. Surrounded by daisies, we sat beside the Kispiox Road and gazed down at the bell tower of the church beside the Skeena. Even from this height we could hear the sound of the river as it rushed past on its long journey to the sea. In the distance the white peaks of the Seven Sisters mountains rose above the valley.

I looked at the sun glistening on Dawn's long black hair. Her Native name means "beauty that came into the world at dawn," and I've always thought how perfectly that suited her. But today she wasn't herself at all.

"Does it really matter all that much?" I asked.

"What do you mean?"

"Well, I've been thinking. Say the mask is never . . ."

"Is never found?" Dawn shuddered. "Graham, don't even think that!"

"But it's just a . . . an *object*. At least you're still alive, Dawn. What if that guy had shot you?"

"I almost wish he had. Part of my soul died when

the mask was lost. Not because I ignored all the warnings when I borrowed it, and not because the mask is worth a lot of money." For a moment Dawn was silent, looking at the Seven Sisters outlined against the blue sky. "I'm proud of my heritage, Graham. The mask binds me to the people who have gone before."

A huge logging truck came toward us, its engine roaring, and I watched the big wheels warily until they'd thundered past. When dust was no longer swirling around us, I looked at Dawn. "I guess it was more to you than a thing. Sort of like . . . losing someone close to you?"

She nodded.

"Then I guess I kind of do understand how you feel."

I leaned back on my elbows and studied the view, watching a couple riding past on bicycles. They wore brightly coloured crash helmets and had a baby who was also decked out in a helmet. They all smiled at us—even the baby—and then I saw Ezra's car heading our way.

Minutes later the green forest was rolling past as we headed north. Ezra's a strong and silent type, so it didn't bother me that he didn't say much, but he seemed a little tense. His knuckles were white on the wheel, and there were lines around his eyes.

"Sold any masks lately, Ezra?"

He shrugged. "A few."

"What about that American museum that was going to show your stuff?"

"The deal fell through. I got a phone call from Boston to say I need time to mature as an artist. They'll take another look at my work in a couple more years."

"That's pretty good news, isn't it?"

"No. I want to succeed *now*. Not when I'm an old man."

"Well, I may not know much about art, but I think your masks and jewellery are fantastic." I looked at the silver bracelet on Dawn's wrist. It showed an intricate design of killer whales. "That bracelet you did for Dawn's birthday is beautiful."

"Thanks, Graham. But I'm afraid the movers and shakers of the art world don't have your good taste. They wouldn't know art if it hit them in the face."

He really booted it after we'd passed through Kispiox and reached the road leading to the rodeo grounds. It's not like him to drive fast, and I was pretty jittery by the time we approached the rodeo.

Normally the rodeo grounds are deserted—just wild flowers and tall grass beside the empty wooden stands and a couple of deserted refreshment booths. But today half the population of the valley was there. Pickups and campers were parked under the trees and all along the river bank. Some people sat in lawn chairs on the roofs of their campers, soaking up the sun and listening to boom boxes, but most of the others were jammed into the stands. I could hear an announcer's excited voice and saw dust rising into the air from the infield, so I was impatient to get a look at the action. I jumped out of the car as soon as Ezra pulled to a stop, but Dawn stayed inside staring at the windshield. Then Ezra said something to her in the Gitksan language and she climbed out, looking close to tears.

"Cheer up," I said. "People are here to enjoy the rodeo. Nobody will say a word about the mask."

She glanced at me with a tiny smile, then stared at the ground. Ezra put an arm around her shoulders and smiled at me. "Thank you for being such a good friend to my sister. It's sad that people have turned against her."

"But I can't understand *why*. She just made a simple mistake."

"That's human nature, Graham. Lots of people need someone to pick on so they can feel better about their own faults. Dawn is a handy target, but I still didn't think there'd be this kind of reaction. It's rough."

I looked toward the stands. "Don't worry about people, Dawn. Besides, everyone's so caught up in the rodeo they'll hardly notice you're here."

"Graham's right." Ezra smiled at his sister. "Now, go have a good time."

Dawn didn't look very enthusiastic, but I was sure the supercharged atmosphere of the rodeo would cheer her up. Everyone was in such a good mood that it was like a party, with some people sitting around campfires singing country and western songs and others smiling at their kids as they chased each other around or rolled in the grass with their puppies. As we approached the stands a calf being led to the infield broke loose and raced toward the river. People in the stands stood up to watch, laughing, then applauded like crazy when the calf was lassoed by its owner just before it plunged into the water.

We joined some friends in time for the Little Britches calf-riding. We knew most of the competitors, and soon Dawn was right into the spirit of things, cheering as each kid was released from a chute on the back of a calf with only a rope to hold. They usually lost their cowboy hats immediately, and most only lasted a few seconds before being bucked off. As they limped across the field, brushing the dust off their jeans, everyone got loud cheers.

"Is Ezra riding today?" I asked Dawn.

"I don't think so. Why?"

"He's over there with the competitors waiting for the adult events." I pointed at a pack of men who stood near the chutes, laughing together about something. Ezra stood near them, talking intensely to a tall Native I'd never seen before. "Who's he?"

"His name's Dark-Sky Thunder. He's from somewhere on the prairies, Saskatchewan or Manitoba. Isn't he incredibly good looking?"

I had to admit the guy had something. Lean and strong, he wore a braided headband that held thick black hair away from his high forehead. I wondered if I'd ever have the nerve to wear a headband.

"He's all right, I guess. Is he in town for the rodeo?"

"I don't know. He's competing today but I can't see him travelling here just for the rodeo. He arrived about a week ago, and people started talking about him right away. I mean, he is so gorgeous."

I was beginning to dislike Dark-Sky Thunder, especially when I looked around the stands and noticed how many other girls were staring at him. Not to mention grown women who should have known better. By the time the bucking-bronco event was announced I was hoping his horse would toss him through the roof of the refreshment booth but, needless to say, he won easily. After accepting the trophy he gave the crowd a wave that looked pretty arrogant to me, and then signed autographs for a bunch of girls who'd been screaming during his ride like they were at a rock concert.

"I'm surprised he can find headbands big enough to fit," I muttered.

Dawn smiled. "Let's go for a walk."

We went down by the river, where a girl was throwing sticks into the water for her black Lab. Just after it had swum ashore for the last time and shaken itself dry, soaking me in the process, I saw Dad approaching and my heart fell.

He was strolling our way with Virginia Lynch.

I might as well admit that nobody agreed with me when I figured Virginia was after my dad. People like Dawn said she'd only been in Hazelton a few weeks and could hardly have fallen in love, especially when her anthropology kept her so busy. But Dad was really naive about women, and I didn't trust Virginia. Not that I'm against Dad getting involved with someone, but I sure didn't want a stepmother who was tiny and blond and looked young enough to be my sister.

So as they approached I produced a phony wave. "Hi, there, guys!"

Virginia smiled. "I hoped to see you calf-roping, Graham. You'd have taken first prize."

"Sure."

"No, really, I mean it. I saw you dance once and you moved like an athlete. With a bit of training you could be a champion."

Dad grinned. "Listen to the lady, son. She's got a real talent for making a man feel he can do anything. Perhaps I'll get you into a soccer uniform yet."

"Aw, Dad, you know I hate that game."

"I know, and it's a shame." He turned to Dawn. "I heard about the mask, Dawn. I'm sorry." He took her arm and they started walking toward the stands, speaking quietly together. That left me with Virginia, who smiled.

"How's the movie coming along?"

"Okay, I guess. I keep changing the script, but I think the basic story is strong."

"Hazelton seems a strange setting for a horror movie, but I guess I don't know the place as well as you do."

"Ever been up to the cemetery? It's a fantastic setting."

"How so?"

"There are all these old gravehouses! I can see my camera zooming in just as . . ."

"Whoa, slow down!" Virginia laughed. "What's a gravehouse?"

"When a Gitksan chief died in the old days a small house was built over the grave. Inside they put the possessions they thought the chief would need in the journey to the next world. Gravehouses aren't built anymore, but you can still see some in the Hazelton cemetery. They're old and grey and creak in the wind. Can't you just picture a stormy night, thunder crackling across the sky, and the camera slowly zooming in on a gravehouse when suddenly, *BLAM!* there's a flash of lightning and we see a human bat, clinging to the gravehouse roof."

"Are you serious about making this movie?"

"Absolutely. I'm already thinking of ways to finance it."

"Then maybe you should consider the feelings of the Gitksan people. They may be insulted by a human bat leaping around the roofs of their gravehouses."

"Are you calling me selfish?"

She smiled, but there was tension around her eyes. "No, I'm just trying to give you some advice."

"Well, let me give *you* some. Stay away from my dad."

"Why stay away?"

"Because I don't want you for a stepmother."

She laughed. "You're rushing things just a little, aren't you? But I do like your father, and I'll continue seeing him as long as I'm in Hazelton."

I stared at her as the wind lifted blond curls away from her forehead. Suddenly my day was ruined. I wished once again that Virginia Lynch had never set foot in this town.

4

I noticed the suspicious object a few hours later. Dawn and I were back in Old Town, walking to the B.C. Café for milkshakes. The heat was intense, bouncing off the walls of the frontier-style buildings and rising in waves from the pavement. As we passed a parked car I glanced in the window, then grabbed Dawn's arm.

"Look!"

Lying on the back seat was something covered by a beach towel.

"Look at that! What does that lumpy shape look exactly like?"

Dawn leaned close to the window. "You may be right. But why would the thief leave it lying around in a car?"

"I don't know, but I think we should take a look."

I grabbed the door handle, then screamed in pain as a jolt of electricity shot up my arm. People turned to stare as an alarm began ringing under the car's hood and I danced around, rubbing my stinging arm. Then the door of the supermarket burst open and the Einsteins came running out.

"What are you doing?" Ma Einstein demanded. "That's our car you're tampering with."

"What about my arm? I'm ruined for life."

Pa Einstein grinned at me. "A few volts won't hurt you. They'll just put hair on your chest." Taking a radio transmitter from his hip pocket, he touched a button and the alarm fell silent. "We designed this security system ourselves," he said, then glanced at the object hidden under the beach towel. "Trying to steal from us, eh?"

"Of course not. We just wanted to see what's under that towel."

"Why is that?"

"Well, we thought, um . . ."

Dawn looked embarrassed. "Graham thought . . . that is, we thought . . . the raven mask might be under that towel."

"It isn't."

"Can we see?" I put in quickly.

Ma Einstein spoke to Dawn without looking my way. "We are elders of your own clan, Dawn. You should trust our word. If we say that's not your mask, it's not."

Pa Einstein touched a transmitter button and they started back to the market. "It's a good idea to leave the car alone, son, unless you want to be hairier than King Kong."

I looked at Dawn. "Funny guy. What'll we do now?"

"Go get our milkshakes."

"But wait a minute! The mask's right in front of our eyes."

Dawn shook her head. "That can't be it. Like the Einsteins said, they're clan elders. I have to trust them."

"Why don't we phone the police? They can get a search warrant, machine-gun the doors, and drag the mask from the smoking remains of the car."

She smiled. "You just want to try out the scene for your movie."

"Dawn, I'm serious! We've got to do something."

"I'm serious, too. I believe the Einsteins. They would never do something like that."

I scuffed the ground with the toe of my cowboy boot. "You're making a mistake, but I guess there's no way to change your feelings about clan elders. Still, how about if we phone the police and give them an anonymous tip?"

"No way, Graham. Just forget it, okay?"

I stared mournfully at the suspicious object in the car. So near and yet so far. As my brain searched for possible solutions to this dilemma I looked down the street and saw the car of my dreams approaching. Inside were Ray West and Grace Heslin. "Here's our chance," I said, waving the car over. "Just a hint about the mask and let them do the rest. Please, Dawn!"

"If you say one word, Graham, I'll never speak to you again."

I looked at her angry dark eyes, the silver medallion at her throat and the sunlight on her long hair. No mask was worth it. As the car pulled to a stop I smiled at Ray.

"I just wanted to say hello."

The man flashed a big grin. "You two want to ride out to the rodeo?"

"No, thanks. We just came from there."

"You still want to buy my car?"

I smiled. "I was only joking. I can hardly afford my bike."

"Keep dreaming big. You'll get to the top one day."

Grace looked at Dawn. "Don't forget our dance rehearsal this evening. There's a lot of work to do."

"Sure, okay."

"You don't sound very enthusiastic."

"I'll be there." Dawn watched the car pull away, then added, "Maybe."

"Are you going to skip the rehearsal?"

"I haven't decided."

"You've never missed one before."

"Things were different before."

I glanced at her, trying to decide when a friend speaks up and when he keeps quiet. Her face was so unhappy that I wished I had the courage to put my arm around her. Instead I grinned. "Come on, let's pig out on milkshakes."

The interior of the B.C. Café was cool. A couple of logger-types sat over coffees at the counter but all the tables were empty so we chose one near the juke box. On the walls were sepia-coloured photographs showing the paddlewheelers that brought cargo and passengers up the rocky canyons of the Skeena River until the railroad was punched through and put them out of business. Mom had read a lot about those days and told me once about a paddlewheeler that sank in a canyon with the loss of five lives and gold worth seventy thousand dollars. The gold had never been recovered, and I sometimes dreamed of going after it.

Our shakes arrived in tall glasses beaded with sweat. I took a long drag on my straw, feeling the smooth liquid slide down my throat and spread in cold waves through my body. "Isn't food a wonderful invention?" I said, sucking up more.

A tiny woman came into the café with her husband. They put some money into the juke box, then ordered coffees and lit cigarettes. I formed my hands into a camera lens and did a slow pan across the café, taking in the long counter, the cash register and the front door just as two familiar faces appeared.

"Don't look now," I whispered, leaning over my milkshake, "but we've got company."

Dawn nodded. "Connor Gentry and Dark-Sky Thunder. I wonder why those two are together? They seem an unlikely combination."

I snuck a look at Connor, taking in his earring and the open shirt revealing his brown chest. "Is he a rodeo rider?"

"Are you kidding? He wouldn't have the stamina for it. He smokes too much."

"Then what's he doing with Dark-Sky Thunder?"

"It beats me."

I switched my attention to Dark-Sky Thunder, examining his clothes and watch and cowboy boots. Then he noticed me staring.

"That guy is mean," I whispered. "He just gave me a look that would vaporize a missile."

"Then quit staring. It's rude."

"I guess I'm tense about the mask. I'd like to nail the person who stole it." I looked at Dark-Sky Thunder. "Maybe he's involved."

"Then why's he still around? Why hasn't he skipped town with the mask?"

"Maybe he's planning to rob some other artifacts from the museum."

I began to get excited about my theory. "He might be the person who tried to break in there, then decided to rob the mask while you danced."

Dawn looked thoughtful. "I did notice him in the audience the night before the robbery."

"That's it then! Let's tell the police."

Dawn shook her head. "Don't be dumb. We don't have a shred of evidence against Dark-Sky Thunder. We're just guessing."

I sat back in my chair, disappointed but also relieved. I really didn't want to get involved, especially since my arm still stung from the Einsteins' booby-trap. Still, I couldn't help feeling curious about the quiet conversation between the two men.

"You know something strange? Connor just happened to be outside your house twice last night."

"What's so strange about that?"

"He doesn't even live near you, so why was he around?"

"Visiting friends, I guess."

"A curious coincidence." I sucked up the last of my milkshake. "Doesn't he live near Hagwilget?"

Dawn nodded. "He's got a house overlooking the canyon. The view's spectacular."

"How do you know?"

She laughed. "Graham, you're so jealous. Connor doesn't interest me."

"You didn't answer my question."

"Ezra took me there once, dummy. He was going to discuss a carving project with Connor and thought I'd like to see the house."

"What's it like?"

"Pretty fancy, actually. He's spent a lot of money installing a skylight and things like that."

"I wouldn't mind seeing it. Want to ride out there on our bikes?"

She looked at me with suspicious eyes. "Why this sudden interest in architecture?"

"I don't know. Maybe there's a raven transformation mask hanging on those fancy walls."

"So you haven't quite lost interest in detective work."

"Maybe we . . ." I paused as the men got up from their table. Dark-Sky Thunder went to pay the bill, and Connor walked our way. A cigarette dangled from his lips, the smoke making him squint. "What're you doing next weekend, Dawn?"

"I don't know. Maybe looking for the mask."

His eyes flickered. "Someone so good-looking shouldn't have been so dumb."

"I don't think you really care about the mask. You just want to give me a rough time."

"You know something? You're wrong. I *do* care about it, more than you'll ever guess." For a long moment he stared at Dawn, then turned and left the café.

I shook my head. "Boy, is he hostile! That guy's just perfect for the role of human bat."

"Let's get out of here, Graham."

"Sounds good."

As we headed for the door a bunch of kids came in. They were all in school with us, and right away I sensed trouble. "Dawn," one of the boys said, "you're just too smart for your own good. Had to be a hotshot and dance with the family mask, didn't you? Now look at the trouble you've caused."

"My father says you shouldn't be allowed to dance anymore," a girl added.

"Then maybe I won't," Dawn said angrily. "Who cares, anyway?"

"Why did you turn over the mask so easily?"

"You were there. You saw Bear wave that gun in my face."

"People are saying you'll make a lot of money when the mask is sold."

"Well, people are crazy. You know those are lies, Marcia, I can tell from your eyes. You just like to get in on good gossip."

I stared at their angry faces, feeling miserable. I wanted to defend Dawn but couldn't think of any words to use. Finally she grabbed my arm and headed for the door. The moment we were outside tears rolled down her cheeks.

"It's not possible, Graham. Why are they so mean?"

"Like Ezra said, picking on you makes people feel better about their own faults."

"I've got to do something. I can't just sit around anymore."

"Sure, but what?"

"I'm going to find the mask."

"Don't take any chances."

"I won't." Dawn wiped her eyes, then ran a hand through her hair. "Listen, one thing you said made sense."

"Only one thing? Thanks a lot."

She smiled. "It *was* strange that Connor was near my house last night. Maybe he was visiting friends, maybe not. I think I'll ride my bike out to his place and ask some questions."

"Sounds like a good idea. I'll come too."

"I can handle Connor. He wouldn't hurt a fly."

"Maybe, but I want to go with you."

"Why?"

"Because it's a beautiful day, and I wouldn't mind a bike ride. Besides, I've never seen a house with a sky-light."

"You're probably wasting your time."

"Let me worry about that. This could be a great adventure, and I'm way overdue for an adventure."

* * *

Soon after, we were riding our bikes along the road to Hagwilget. We passed a scattering of houses and a girl riding a horse, but mostly there were only trees and fields to look at. As we rode past a pond I saw some Canada geese paddling across the still water, then a red-winged blackbird flew to a telephone line to sound a shrill warning.

When we approached a sign reading *One-Lane Bridge Ahead* I started getting nervous, because of the fatal flaw in my character. Heights left me a blubbering idiot, and the suspension bridge at Hagwilget was an absolute killer. I'd remembered it before we left Old Town, but maybe I was too embarrassed to say anything to Dawn. Now we were approaching the bridge and I knew my fear hadn't changed.

Goosebumps like rocks rose on my skin as we glimpsed the bridge above the trees, the long support cables rising to the top of steel towers. I got so shaky I thought I'd fall off my bike. On the far side of the canyon the houses of Hagwilget clustered around a white church. I remembered Mom saying that the Wet'suwet'en Natives built the first bridge across the canyon by stringing rope made of cedar bark from support poles. She said it hung in the air like a spider's web but was perfectly safe. Just the thought of it gave me the creeps.

The so-called modern bridge didn't look much safer. The Bulkley River was visible far below, squeezed between narrow canyon walls. The water was churned into white foam as it raged past boulders and through rapids, then flowed into an open area where it swirled around in patterns that reflected the sunlight. After that the river was lost from sight as it continued its journey to the place near 'Ksan where it joins the Skeena.

Slowly I pushed my bike out onto the narrow bridge. As I did, a big transport came down the hill at Hagwilget and roared onto the bridge. The deck began to shake and tremble. Then the iron cables groaned as the bridge swayed under the weight of the truck. I retreated fast, reaching safety just before the transport roared past.

"Are you okay?" Dawn asked. "You're so white."

The pity in her voice made me feel like crawling under a rock. Climbing onto my bike, I took a deep breath and raced out on the bridge. As I did I looked down, and for a moment I thought I'd faint at the sight of the leaping white water so far below. Then I fixed my eyes on the far side of the bridge and raced forward.

My heart leapt when the bike wheels touched the firm pavement of the road. "I can't believe it!" I dropped my bike and did a crazy dance all around the road, then saw another transport approaching and I just got my bike to safety before it was squashed. Feeling I could climb Mt. Everest without flinching, I grinned at Dawn.

"Where's that million-dollar house?"

"Just beyond these woods."

We ditched our bikes near a trail and followed it through the trees. Flies and mosquitoes attacked our heads, but I hardly noticed because I was feeling so good. Within minutes we reached the last trees and saw a house in an open field. The walls had once been white but now were grey. Holes showed in the roof. Swallows flew in and out the empty windows, which showed the black interior.

"That is Connor Gentry's house?"

"I thought you'd be more impressed. Notice the many skylights which let in the sun."

"And the rain. What's going on?"

"Look over there." Smiling, Dawn pointed toward the canyon where a modern house stood above the roaring river. It was small, but the walls were made of beautiful wood and a large skylight reflected the bright sunlight.

"If that's Connor's house, what's the other dump?"

"Some place that's been deserted for years. I thought we could hide in it and see what happens at Connor's."

"Weren't you going to ask him some questions?"

"Yeah, but now I can't think of any. I'm no Sherlock Holmes, I guess."

"Neither am I." I studied Connor's house. "How could he afford a place like that?"

"His mother lives in Prince Rupert. People say she won a lottery and gave him half."

"Do you think that's true?"

"Who knows?"

Trying to avoid being spotted by Connor, we bent low while running across the field toward the wrecked house. Wind gusted through the tall grass, and bees worked busily among the purple fireweed flowers that seemed to grow everywhere. We ran up the porch steps and hurried inside, hearing broken glass crunch underfoot.

"Listen to the creepy noise the wind makes blowing through here," I said. "This is an excellent setting for my film! Why'd you keep it from me?"

The floor was made of bare planks but some had been ripped away and the ground was visible through the gaps. I looked in some swallow nests at their tiny speckled eggs, then glanced at an old chair leaning against a wall. A breeze came through the window to stir the chunks of insulation that hung from the ceiling.

For a long time we stood at a window watching Connor's house. After I'd memorized every detail of the walls, the roof, the chimney, the skylight and the door I began to wonder if he was even home. Finally I gave up and began wandering around. I took another look at the swallows' nests, then found a place where stairs had once led to the upper floor. The broken wall was easy to climb and within seconds I was walking around upstairs. There wasn't much to see except the holes in the roof and the swallows outside the empty windows, wheeling and crying as they waited for us to leave. I walked to a window at the back of the house and shielded my eyes against the sunshine. On the far side of the field was a tent. I saw a man beside it.

At the same moment, the man saw me.

Even though we were separated by an entire field, I could feel the force of his eyes. Then he started across the field in my direction, and I started running.

"Dawn," I yelled. "Let's get out of here!"

Grabbing the wall, I went down it in double-fast time. Dawn stood at the bottom, staring at me. "Don't ask questions," I shouted. "Just run!"

"What?"

"It's Dark-Sky Thunder, and he's coming this way!"

Glass broke under our feet like gunshots as we scrambled across the porch and reached the fireweed. Dark-Sky Thunder yelled at us to stop but we just kept moving, smashing through the tall grass. From behind came the sound of feet, and I knew that Dark-Sky Thunder was gaining as we reached the path through the trees.

"Hurry, Graham! If we can get to our bikes we'll be okay!"

But when we reached them my hands were shaking so badly I couldn't hold my bike steady. As I tried to control it I heard Dark-Sky Thunder coming along the path, yelling for us to stop. Overwhelmed by panic, I dropped the bike and ran toward the bridge. The single word *escape!* screamed inside my head as I dashed along the metal deck.

Then I saw the logging truck.

It was heading onto the bridge. The headlights were on high-beam, glaring at me. It was piled high with huge logs that would crush me to a pulp. The engine thundered as the driver geared down, trying to stop, and then the horn blared.

I knew the truck could never stop in time. Throwing myself toward the side of the bridge I scrambled over the railing and landed on a small platform. Grabbing a support cable I hung on tight as the logging truck roared past, shaking the bridge and sending violent ripples through the cable.

Moaning, I gripped the cable. Then I glimpsed the churning white water far below. As an anguished cry escaped from my lips I heard Dark-Sky Thunder's deep voice.

"You're okay, kid. Let go of the cable and grab the railing."

But I couldn't move.

"Come on, kid, I know you can make it."

Very slowly I turned my head in his direction. Dawn and Dark-Sky Thunder leaned over the railing, staring at me. Then a man ran to join them. "I was driving the truck," he said. "Is that boy crazy?"

Dark-Sky Thunder climbed over the railing and

dropped to the platform beside me. There was a strength about him that gave me confidence, but I still couldn't release my grip. Dark-Sky Thunder's hand took mine, then he pulled it loose from the support cable.

Tearing my other hand free, he spun my body toward the railing and lifted me across it with powerful arms. The truck driver grabbed me, then I collapsed on the bridge deck.

I was safe, but I felt like a jerk.

5

The next day I was still feeling terrible. Just when I'd finally overcome my fear of heights I ended up hanging over the river expecting to die. If Dark-Sky Thunder hadn't been there, what would have happened?

The thought put me into another cold sweat. I kept picturing the white water so far below the bridge, then Dark-Sky Thunder's angry face after he'd got me to safety. He'd wanted to know why we'd been spying on him, but I was too emotionally wrecked to answer and Dawn just ignored his questions.

Again I shook my head, trying to clear away the bad memories. I had come to the Hazelton graveyard to put some flowers on my mother's grave, and now I stood beside it looking at the massive shape of Stek'yaw'den. Shadowed by the morning sun it rose huge against the sky. I studied it through my camera-lens hands, then panned down past Mom's grave to a wide-angle shot of the graveyard. Wild grass grew tall, and the only sound came from the wind rustling the poplars. Old and rickety gravehouses stood where chiefs had been buried in the old days, and weathered fences surrounded other graves. I zoomed in on a white tombstone placed on the back of a large stone frog, then cut to one carved in the shape of a raven.

I looked at the cross on Mom's grave, picturing her face and her smile. To tell the truth it kind of tortured me to visit here, but I still came almost every day. I walked to the fence that surrounded the graveyard and looked down the hill to the streets of Hazelton. I could see kids playing in their yards and heard the barking of dogs, and somehow that made me feel better. Then I looked at the white tower of the church by the river and my stomach clenched when I thought about Virginia. I needed her in my life like I needed a hole in the head.

The hot sunshine felt good as I wandered through the graveyard in the direction of the Kispiox Road. But when I glanced at my watch I got a shock. I was late for my meeting with Ezra.

"Oh, no," I muttered, breaking into a run.

Ezra had promised me a day of fly-fishing and now I'd blown it. I dashed down the long road from the cemetery, but there was no sign of Ezra. I paced beside the road, wondering what to do, then saw the car of my dreams approaching. I waved my arms and heaved a sigh of relief when Ray West, the museum curator, pulled over.

"Hi, Graham, where are you bound?"

"I'm late meeting Ezra. He's taking me fishing on the Kispiox River. Are you heading that way?"

"Sure thing. I'll open the sunroof and crank up the music."

"Fantastic! I just hope Ezra will be waiting for me out there." I grinned as my body settled back on the ultimate luxury of calfskin. With a surge of power the car pulled away. Sweet-smelling air poured through the sunroof, but it was so perfectly designed that not a hair moved on my head.

"When my dad's got the windows open it's like a tornado blowing through. Our car's a bit of a wreck, to tell the truth."

"Ministers don't make much money, but I guess they're happy."

"You must do okay as a museum curator."

"I get by." He smiled. "I'm a happy bachelor, so my salary goes on this machine and the beauties who ride inside it."

I looked at his dark hair and wide mouth, envying his lifestyle. He reminded me of those young guys you see on police shows, having a great time in between racing around catching crooks.

"You should live in Miami or somewhere like that."

He laughed. "Life's not so bad in Hazelton."

"I guess I'll be leaving some day. I'm going to shoot my first film here, then search for other locations." For a few minutes I studied the car's displays and leather-wrapped steering wheel, then looked sideways at Ray.

"What do you think of Dawn as a dancer?"

"She's the best. I've never seen such talent."

"That's exactly what I think!"

"Got a bit of a crush on her?"

I shrugged. "Maybe."

"She's a beautiful young lady."

"Sure, but it's not just her looks. I feel good when I'm with her, know what I mean?"

"Some ladies of my acquaintance affect me that way."

"But I feel I'm not getting anywhere with Dawn. I wish I was like that guy Dark-Sky Thunder. She thinks he's *gorgeous*. Anyway, I figure my only hope is to find that mask and be a hero in her eyes."

Ray glanced at me. "Any chance of you tracking it down?"

"I don't know. I've got a couple of ideas."

"Such as?"

"Well . . ." I thought about the Einsteins and my suspicions, but it didn't seem fair to mention them. "I'd better not say anything."

Again he looked at me. "Let the police do the investigating, Graham."

"You're right. But there must be some other way to dazzle Dawn."

"Maybe you're trying too hard."

"What do you mean?"

"You and Dawn may only ever be friends." He smiled. "Hey, don't look so down. If it doesn't work out with Dawn, your time will come with someone else. You've got a lot going for you, kid."

"Oh, yeah? I'm not *gorgeous* like Dark-Sky Thunder."

"So what? Look around at married couples and what do you see? Normal-looking people. In the end it's the personality inside you that counts. All those ordinary people found someone who loved their jokes or their tenderness or whatever."

"But that's in the future. What about *now*?"

"Be patient. When I was in grade nine nobody would date me. Finally I gave up trying and got involved in things I enjoyed. Skiing trips and the school band and stuff like that. All of a sudden I started meeting girls who played the trombone or were great skiers. Pretty soon I was legendary for the females in my life."

"That all sounds great, but I only want to be a legend to Dawn."

After Ray dropped me off near the rodeo grounds, I walked over to the river. Ezra wasn't around and for a moment I thought he'd left without me. But there was no sign of his car and I knew he always started his fishing expeditions from the rodeo grounds, so I hoped he was late, too. I decided to sit down and wait. With luck he'd turn up before long.

The voices of yesterday's crowd echoed inside my head like ghosts. I looked at the empty chutes and deserted infield, then at the heat rising from the grey fence around the stands. All around me the buttercups were such an intense colour they stung my eyes. Leaning back, I turned my face to the sun.

The air was so clean it had a sweet taste. I could hear the cool, liquid gush of the river as a breeze shivered the leaves of the cottonwoods along its banks. I was so relaxed in the burning sun that I was beginning to fall asleep, so I stood up and went exploring.

Above my head swallows were preening themselves on power lines leading to two small log buildings. I glanced in the open door of the one that had been used yesterday as a refreshment stand, then wandered on to the second. It had probably been a food stand in other years because I saw a big stove and shelves for supplies, but it looked abandoned. Dust was everywhere, and swallow nests lined the log walls.

The inside of the building was cool after the intense heat of the sun. Leaning against a table, I watched the swallows flit through the open windows. Then I heard something that made my skin prickle.

A motorcycle was approaching.

I knew it couldn't be Ezra because he drove a car. I guess my nerves were on edge because of what had been happening, so I felt suddenly afraid. Spotting a stack of old cartons, I slipped behind them.

Within seconds I heard the sound of feet. Then someone crossed the wooden floor and the oven door squealed. Moments later the motorcycle roared back to life.

Scrambling out of hiding, I ran to a window in time to see the motorcycle racing away.

The rider was Connor Gentry.

* * *

What had he been doing? I looked inside the oven. It was empty, but there were marks in the dust. There'd been saddlebags on the motorcycle, so maybe Connor had come here for something that had been hidden inside the stove.

I couldn't wait to pass this news on to Ezra.

Eventually he arrived, but he climbed so wearily from his car that I decided to keep quiet.

"Sorry I'm late," Ezra said. "When you weren't

waiting near the cemetery I figured you'd found another ride out here." He began unloading fishing gear from the car and gave me two pairs of wool socks plus layers of thermal clothing.

"We'll need this protection standing in the cold water, otherwise our body heat would drain away."

"Is something wrong? You seem kind of quiet."

"I just had a major argument with a man I don't like. That's why I'm late."

"I was afraid you were mad because I wasn't waiting near the graveyard. Ray West came along and I couldn't resist a ride in that car of his."

"I hope you don't grow up in love with money, Graham. Your mother wasn't like that, and neither's your dad."

"Hey, as long as I can have my beach house at Malibu, I won't ask for anything more."

"You're joking, right?"

"Come on. I'm just trying to cheer you up, Ezra."

But he just stared at the jade-green waters of the Kispiox. "I've always wanted to teach you something about fly-fishing, partly as a way of repaying your mother. She was my mentor."

"What does that mean?"

"She taught me about fly-fishing. Remember how much she loved it?"

"Sure. She had that little workshop in our basement where she tied flies. She even designed her own."

"I've always thought that someday I'd teach you to love it, too. Then that part of your mother would live on inside you." Ezra shook his head. "But time's running out."

We inflated a rubber raft with a foot pump, loaded our supplies and pushed off from shore. The swift water carried us quickly away from the rodeo grounds. Except for the liquid rush of the river along the rocky shoreline, we entered a world that was utterly silent. Everything was green: the emerald river, the tall cottonwoods along the riverbank, and the willows, birch, poplar and spruce that seemed to grow everywhere.

Ezra used small oars to keep us in the middle of the stream. "There are only certain places along the Kispiox that are good for fly-fishing, Graham. I'm taking you to the best one."

I watched a sandpiper speed across the river, twisting and darting above the surface like a jet fighter, then looked up at a raven flapping across the blue sky. "I've got to tell you something, Ezra."

"What's that?"

I turned to him. "I think Connor Gentry has the raven mask."

His eyes narrowed. "Why?"

Quickly I described what had happened at the log building. "I think he ditched the mask inside the stove, then got it today. It would be a perfect hiding place."

Ezra didn't reply. Instead he concentrated his attention on the oars as we swept around a small, rocky island and then approached a cottonwood that had fallen into the river. "Look at how its bark has been stripped away by beavers."

"Are there any around here?"

"Sure. Haven't you been watching them?"

I shook my head, feeling dumb. Ezra's sharp eyes were probably picking out a million details I was missing. I looked straight down into the water, hoping to find a beaver, then stared at the shore in hopes of seeing one bringing down a tree with its teeth. But I couldn't see a thing.

"Over there, Graham."

Ezra pointed at a log near the riverbank. For a moment I saw nothing, then my heart jumped when I spotted a chubby little beaver resting on the log. "It hasn't seen us," Ezra whispered. The beaver slipped into the water and swam downstream with its head showing, then suddenly noticed us. With a loud *SLAP!* of its tail it dived beneath the surface.

Ezra laughed. "They go down like submarines." He pointed to a pile of sticks heaped together near the bank. "There's a beaver house."

"Wow. I've never seen a beaver this close before. Are we going to see anything else?"

"If we're lucky."

"Ezra, what should I do about Connor Gentry? Report him to the Mounties?"

"You don't have any evidence except a few scuff marks inside a dusty stove."

"What about the way he's been picking on Dawn? I bet he's stirring up people against her to cover his own guilt."

"If you take that evidence to the police they'll laugh you out of their office." Ezra shook his head. "Don't start playing detective. I'm not, and neither is Dawn."

"She is so. Didn't she mention what happened yesterday?"

I told him about going to Connor's place, and about being rescued by Dark-Sky Thunder at the suspension bridge. Ezra's black eyes watched me carefully.

"I think I should ground Dawn until our folks get home. It might be smart for your dad to do the same."

"What do you mean?"

"Look, Graham, the theft of the raven mask is a serious business. The people involved could be dangerous. If you and my sister keep playing detective, someone may get hurt."

"We're not playing, Ezra. We're trying to help."

"Well, just forget it. Do you hear me, Graham? Forget it!"

For a moment I tried to hold his eyes, then I looked toward the riverbank. Who did he think he was? For a minute I felt like chucking the whole fishing trip. I mean, I knew Ezra was worried about Dawn, but he didn't need to treat us like babies. As I sulked I watched a kingfisher power low across the river. Then I looked downstream and got the shock of my life.

A bear.

It was standing near a pile of logs on shore, digging under some bushes with its paw. "Ezra, look," I whispered. As we drifted closer I heard the sudden *SLAP!* of a beaver tail and saw the bear raise its head. It peered our way with tiny eyes, then crashed away through the bushes. I listened to its noisy escape, then turned to Ezra.

"Wow!"

He smiled. "Some sight, eh?"

"I can't believe I saw a real bear!"

Ezra nodded. "They're magnificent creatures and a

really important part of my people's lives. At Kitwancool there's a totem pole that tells how a grizzly swam the river carrying her cubs on each side of her head. When she got into swift waters she lost one of the cubs and it drowned. Afterwards she cried for her baby. Her song of mourning has been sung by my people ever since. Whenever I'm on the river I think of the sadness of that grizzly."

I stared at the bushes where the bear had disappeared. "Sometimes, in the middle of the night, I lie in bed crying about Mom. Last month I smashed up a model car she gave me at Christmas."

"Now and then you have to let out your anger and pain, Graham. That's why the grizzly sang her death song and why my people grieve openly when they've lost someone."

We drifted in silence until Ezra pulled the raft up on a low gravel bar. We unloaded our supplies and then put on chestwaders. "This is a good spot, Graham, because there's fast water at the head of the gravel, then the river slows down and gets deeper. At the bottom are boulders that provide shelter where the fish can rest."

"Are we going after steelhead?"

"You bet. That's what the Kispiox is famous for. It holds the world record for the largest steelhead ever taken on a fly."

"A steelhead's a salmon, right?"

"Wrong. It's a sea-going trout. They're good fighters, which is why people come from all over the world to fish the Kispiox. But the challenge also lies in knowing enough about the fish, and flies, to be able to land one. Did you know there are more books written about fly-fishing than any other sport?"

We waded out until the bottom beneath our feet changed from sand to rocks. The water sucked and swirled around our legs, but the thermal clothing and double wool socks kept us warm. "The fish lie close in to that shore," Ezra said, pointing to the far bank which was shaded by cottonwoods. "Cast into the current and let it carry the fly downstream."

The pole was light in my hands. The fly-fishing I'd watched on television looked easy, but it took a lot of practice before I could make the fly do anything for me. As I worked at it, Ezra used effortless motions to cast flies exactly where he wanted them.

Suddenly a fish broke the surface. Its silver body flashed in the sunlight and then it was under again, running with the line. "Quickly," Ezra said, handing me the pole, "follow my instructions as you fight it." With a pounding heart I watched the line race from the reel, then go slack. "Reel in now, Graham!" I reeled, then felt the steelhead turn and run again. "Stay with it! You've got to tire the fish. This one's a real fighter."

Again the line went slack and I reeled in desperately, groaning as my muscles ached. I was beginning to think the fight would last forever, but I stayed with it and eventually watched, breathless, as Ezra slid the steelhead from the river. Water streamed from its lean body and I could see the blue colouring on its head that gave the fish its name.

"She's a beauty," Ezra said, carefully removing the hook from its mouth. "Want to release her to fight another day?"

For a moment I hesitated. Then I nodded. "Let her go."

"Good man." Ezra held the steelhead in the water until her strength came back. Then with a flick of her tail she was gone. "You did a nice job, Graham. Congratulations."

"Thanks! That was fantastic."

Back at the gravel bar we peeled off the waders. My body was tired but I tingled with pleasure at what I'd accomplished. As Ezra built a small fire I walked to the end of the bar and stood by a log watching the river bubble past. With my camera-lens hands I studied some ducks swimming along the far bank and then slowly panned to Ezra leaning over the fire. The scene was perfectly back-lit by the slanting sunshine. I guess I'd never felt happier.

"Ezra," I said, walking over to him, "I just want to say thanks. It's been a perfect day."

"Let's hope we can do it again."

"Maybe I can give you a part in my film. You know, to sort of return the favour."

He poured out tea that was hot and good. With it we ate fried bread covered in apricot jam. The smell of cottonwood pollen was in the air, and a kingfisher chattered from its perch overlooking the water.

"Ezra, do you think I'm crazy?"

"Not usually. What do you mean?"

"I don't know. Maybe a kid from Hazelton can't grow up to be a film director. Maybe I'm dumb to think I can actually make it in a place like Hollywood."

Sipping his tea, Ezra looked at the green water. "Never lose faith in yourself. I haven't, and I never will. If that Boston museum won't exhibit my masks, some other place will. I won't quit until I'm recognized internationally."

"You will be, Ezra. Your work is great."

"You make a good cheering section, Graham. So was your mother. She told me to be patient, but I'm just not that kind of guy."

"I know the feeling." Again I did a camera study of the beautiful scene. The smooth pebbles on the riverbed rattled together as the river flowed swiftly past. I wanted time to stand still. "My mom always used to tell me not to be in such a hurry for things. I guess I never listened the way I should have."

"Your mother was one of those people who make the world a richer place. Simon Gun'an'noot was like that, too. I've tried to find strength in his example."

"Who was he?"

"People called him the Phantom of the Kispiox. He was accused of murder but there was no real evidence. Gun'an'noot was afraid of what might happen in the white man's court so he hid out in the wilderness for thirteen years." Ezra looked at the river, then the distant mountains. "Gun'an'noot was a trapper and a very powerful man. His Native name meant 'young bears that run up trees.' The search for him was the most expensive in the history of British Columbia. The government even brought in the Pinkerton Detective Agency, but they failed, too."

Ezra paused, looking at the forest. "I often wonder if Gun'an'noot once hid among these very trees, watching a police patrol pass by. He knew this land so well that he continued to trap, and he often slipped past the police to take furs to his family in Kispiox.

When his father died, Gun'an'noot carried him on his back seventy kilometres to the lake where he'd asked to be buried. Finally Gun'an'noot came into contact with a lawyer who convinced him to stand trial. When the case went to a jury he was found not guilty." For several minutes Ezra was silent. Then he stared at me with those fierce eyes. "I wish I had that kind of spirit!"

I shook my head. "You could hide out for thirty years, Ezra. I bet you know this country as well as Gun'an'noot."

"I doubt it, but maybe someday I'll have to learn."

6

By the time I got home from the fishing trip the church bell was calling people to evening service. The sound was deep and rich. Dad once climbed the series of ladders inside the tower and discovered the bell was made by an English company in 1902. Later he learned it was brought here from the coast in a Haida war canoe. Sometimes I've wished I could have seen the inscription on the bell, but my fear of heights has killed that idea.

Dawn always attended Sunday evening service with me, so I waited on the riverbank for her. In the distance the sun slid behind the mountains, turning them black beneath the pale blue of the sky. The moment the sun disappeared the air turned cold.

"Hi, Graham." I turned to see Dawn. She gave me a

faint smile and then looked at the rushing water. "How was your fishing trip?"

"Great! I actually caught a steelhead. I wish you'd been there."

"I should have gone. I just hung around the house all day."

"What about your dance rehearsal?"

"I skipped it."

"Again? That's two in a row, and you've never missed a rehearsal in your life."

"Don't nag me about this, Graham."

"Are people still giving you a rough time?"

"Of course."

"Then why don't we do something about the mask?"

"Like what?"

I stared at the water, trying to think. "The mask could still be somewhere around Hazelton. If so, who's got it? We've already checked out Connor Gentry and . . ."

"And that was a flop."

"Sure, but what about the Einsteins?"

"We've already discussed this, Graham. The Einsteins are elders of my clan and, besides, they don't need money. Why steal the mask?"

"I bet there's a secret motive. I'm sure that was the mask on the back seat of their car. Otherwise why the fancy alarm system that fried my arm?"

"The Einsteins are like that. Always tinkering with alarms and computers and stuff."

I looked carefully at Dawn. "I need to know more about the Einsteins. Wish me luck."

"What are you talking about?"

"I'm going out to their place tonight. With luck I'll

spot the raven mask through a window."

"That's crazy."

"The police haven't learned anything, so I guess it's up to me."

"You're going there tonight?"

"Yup." I did my best to look heroic. "By tomorrow my name will be on everyone's lips. 'Local boy cracks case' or something like that. Maybe you should get an autograph now before I get too busy with interviews."

She rolled her eyes and sighed. "Then I'd better go with you."

"But the Einsteins are your clan elders."

"I know that, and I know they're not guilty. But someone has to keep an eye on you."

After church we went to the vicarage, where Dad and I lived, for a late supper. As Dad and Virginia prepared the food, Dawn found a magazine in the living-room and I went upstairs to my room. I fed King some almonds and then sat down at my computer. It wasn't anything fancy but it did a nice job. One of the scenes in my film was troubling me, so I was changing the dialogue when there was a tap on the door.

"May I come in?" a voice asked. It was Virginia. For a moment I kept working on my dialogue, then grunted permission.

"I like your room," she said. "Who are those singers in the big poster?"

I looked at her in surprise. "You really don't know?"

Virginia laughed. "I guess I'm a little out of date." She sat on the bed beside King and rubbed him under the chin. The diamonds on her fingers winked in the light. "Graham, I wish we could be friends."

I didn't say anything.

"I like the picture of your mother on top of the computer." For a few seconds she concentrated on King. "I don't want to replace her, you know. I might even be leaving town soon."

"Oh, yeah?"

"It's not definite, but my studies of the Gitksan are pretty well finished."

"Where will you go next?"

"I don't know."

"Hollywood? You're pretty enough."

"Thank you, Graham. What a nice thing to say."

"That's where I'll be eventually."

"I really respect your ambition. When I was your age my big dream was to be a stage designer. I wanted to study theatre in university but my parents said no. I wasn't strong enough to stand up to them and save my dream."

"Do you like being an anthropologist?"

She nodded. "Things are pretty exciting for me, I guess, but sometimes I meet a good person like your dad and I realize my life took a wrong turning somewhere. Then I wish I could start over and not make the same mistakes."

"Next time you'll make different ones?"

"Probably," she said, laughing. She stroked King's head and then stood up. "Well, I was sent up here to say supper's ready. You're probably hungry."

We went downstairs together to the dining room, where Dad and Dawn were talking at the table.

"I went fly-fishing with Ezra today," I announced as I sat down. "I caught a steelhead."

"Congratulations!" Dad grinned at me. "Will we be having fish for breakfast?"

"Nope. We let it go."

Virginia looked up from her soup. "How was Ezra?"

"A little tense at first. He said he had an argument with some guy."

"Did he say why?"

"Nope." I fiddled with my soup, then looked at Dad. "Ever heard of Simon Gun'an'noot?"

"Your mother told me about him." He turned to Virginia. "That's how you and I met, remember? We got talking at the market and I mentioned Dorothy's interest in Gitksan history."

Virginia nodded. "I've learned a lot from her collection of books."

Dad turned to me. "Why did you ask about Gun'an'noot?"

"Ezra says he could never survive in the wilderness like Gun'an'noot. I said that's nuts."

"Ezra's going to hide out in the wilderness?" Virginia asked.

"Of course not. We were just talking."

"Maybe Ezra meant it," Dawn said. "He's been really upset since the mask was stolen. Being my brother has been tough on him."

Dad squeezed her hand. "Don't talk that way, Dawn."

"The mask will turn up," Virginia said. "There can't be many hiding places for something that big. I'm sure the police will figure it all out."

"They're good officers," Dad said. "I understand they're watching that rodeo rider Dark-Sky Thunder. Someone told me he's had a shady past."

Virginia smiled. "You sound like an old gangster movie, Vernon. Anyway, Dark-Sky Thunder couldn't have been wearing the bear regalia the night of the theft. He's far too tall."

"Sure," I said, "but maybe he hired someone to steal the mask."

"Then where is it now?" Dad asked. "And why is Dark-Sky Thunder still hanging around town?"

"Maybe the person he hired has changed his mind. He won't turn over the mask because he wants to sell it himself."

"That's a pretty good theory. You'd make a good detective, Graham."

I grinned. "Maybe you could be one, too. Remember Mom telling us about Doc Wilson? He was a minister, just like you."

"What's this all about?" Virginia asked.

"Hazelton was the scene of the only major gun fight in the history of the Canadian West," Dad explained. "Seven men tried to rob the Union Bank, a little log building that was jammed with the money being earned by construction workers building the railway through here. The robbers were pinned inside the bank by some sharp-shooting locals, including the Presbyterian minister Doc Wilson. I guess they put something like two hundred bullets into the log walls and through the windows. When the robbers made a break for the forest some were picked off by the sharp-shooters and almost all the others were captured soon after."

"And they got the money back?"

Dad shook his head. "One man got away with the

money. The crooks who weren't dead were sentenced to twenty years in prison. So I guess that . . ."

As he paused I smiled at him. "Go ahead, Dad, say it! *So I guess that proves crime doesn't pay.*"

He laughed. "And it doesn't. Even the man who escaped with the loot can't have enjoyed spending it when he thought about his friends lying dead, or stuck behind bars. I'm sure the person who stole the raven mask feels the same way at this very minute. No matter how much money can be made, it's not worth the heartbreak of Dawn and her people."

Virginia stood up. "It's getting late, Vernon. Would you drive me to the rooming house?"

"Of course."

As soon as they'd left, I looked at Dawn. "The time has come. Are you coming with me to the Einsteins' place?"

"I guess so, but I still don't think it's a great idea. We could live to regret this, Graham."

"Not a chance."

* * *

We ditched our bikes in some bushes beside the Kispiox Road. The night was silent and black. A half-moon lit up a sign that read: NO TRESPASSING—YOU HAVE BEEN WARNED.

"Welcome to the Einstein estate," Dawn said. "They certainly make it clear they don't want visitors."

A locked gate guarded the dirt road that twisted away among the trees. To each side of the gate was a high barbed-wire fence. Fearing that the gate might be booby-trapped, we walked slowly along the fence hoping to find an opening. Sure enough, after pushing through the undergrowth for a while, we got lucky.

"Look down there." Dawn pointed at a hollow in the ground. "Some animal dug a hole to get under the fence."

"Do you think it was a dog?" I swallowed. "Maybe a Doberman pinscher, or a German shepherd? Something big and powerful dug that hole. Maybe it's hiding behind one of those trees, waiting for us to crawl under the fence."

Dawn didn't reply. She knelt down, then wiggled through the hollow and came out on the far side of the fence. "It's easy, Graham. There's plenty of room, but don't touch the barbed wire. It might be electrified."

"You mean I'll be sizzled by ten thousand volts?"

"Just be careful."

It would have been easier if Dawn hadn't mentioned electricity. As I knelt down I could feel the sweat running down my body. After working my way under the fence I searched the dark forest for hidden attack dogs, then looked up into the trees. "There could be commandos waiting in those branches. They'll drop down silently as we pass. We'll never know what hit us."

It took a long time to get through the forest. The moonlight was cut off by the tall trees and the undergrowth was incredibly thick. Nettles stung my skin, roots tripped me and branches scratched my face. I was sweaty and tired by the time we reached an open field.

"I can see a light way over there," I whispered, pointing. "It must be the house."

Dawn nodded. "So far, so good."

"You mean so far, no guard dog."

Under the full light of the moon we ran across the field. Dawn was a swift runner and quickly left me behind. She was waiting in the shelter of a wooden fence when I dropped down beside her, gasping for air. "If I smoked, I'd have an excuse for this," I groaned, holding my aching sides. "I guess I'm in terrible shape."

"I've been studying the house. I can't tell if anyone's home."

Cautiously I raised my head above the fence. Close by was a small barnyard with several sheds. A cow stood near one shed, and a white horse stared at me from the middle of the muddy yard. A narrow passage led between the sheds to the dark shape of the house where only a single light shone from an upstairs window. Beyond the house a bluff rose steeply, topped by thick trees.

"We'll be able to get closer to the house if we stick near those sheds." Dawn stood up. "Come on."

"Watch it," I warned as she reached for the fence. "What about the ten thousand volts?"

"In a wooden fence?"

"I guess you're right."

After she climbed the fence I scrambled to the top and jumped down on the other side. A cool breeze touched the sweat on my forehead as we ran to a shed. Now we were close enough to see that the house was made of logs. Moonlight glinted from the dark windows and curtains covered the upstairs window where a light was burning. There was no sign of life.

"Okay," I whispered, "let's get across this open space to the house. Then we'll work our way around to the far side. With luck there'll be lights on in those rooms and we'll be able to see inside."

"And if we don't see the mask, we're going straight home. Right?"

I nodded. "Let's get moving." I started running, then tripped and fell to my knees. They hit something hard, but somehow I kept from yelling out. Dawn helped me up, and I limped beside her to the wall of the house. Except for my fall, it had all been easy.

Too easy.

Suddenly an enormous spotlight switched on. A powerful glare shone on us. Then a second spotlight leapt into life, and a third. The yard and house were lit as if by daylight. Dawn and I were frozen, staring at each other in shock.

"DON'T MOVE," boomed a voice from a hidden loudspeaker. "YOU HAVE BEEN SEEN AND IDEN-TIFIED. RAISE YOUR HANDS."

It was too much for my nerves. They snapped. One second I was looking at Dawn's stunned face, the next second I was running down the narrow passage between the sheds.

From behind, the loudspeaker screamed at me to stop. I ducked my head, expecting bullets to fly. I had almost reached the wooden fence when it happened. Directly in front of me a camouflaged trap door fell open.

I yelled.

I tried to stop.

But it was impossible, and with a sickening cry I plunged into an open pit.

With a tremendous splash, I landed in slimy water. Somehow I kept my head from going under, and thrashed to the side of the pit. Looking up, I saw Dawn running my way.

"Are you okay, Graham?"

"I'm soaked, and this water stinks. Help me out of here!"

Two figures emerged from the house and hurried toward us through the spotlights' glare. The Einsteins were grinning with pleasure.

"Looks like we caught a big one," Ma Einstein said.

Her husband looked down at me. "We spent a long time designing the ultimate burglar-proof house. Thanks for testing our defences."

"Help me out of this disgusting water. Please!"

Chuckling, he reached for my hands. With a powerful heave he pulled me out of the pit.

"You'd better come inside and shower, son. You smell like last week's garbage. Then you two can explain why you invaded our private property."

"Sorry to be a nuisance," I said miserably.

He laughed and slapped my wet back. "Best night of our lives! I'll never forget the way you yelled, just before you dropped into the pit."

Ma Einstein grinned. "We got it all on video. It'll be our favourite late-night show."

I groaned. "That's all I need. Starring on TV as the Hazelton Slime."

7

I felt miserable as I stood in the shower.

I was haunted by the memory of the pit. Worse, I couldn't forget that it was all on video. The recording might also become a Gitksan treasure, passed down from generation to generation. In the twenty-fifth century I'd still be dropping into the filthy water.

Later I sat by the fireplace, wrapped in Pa Einstein's dressing gown. Ma Einstein had run my clothes through the washer and now they were tumbling in the dryer. She'd had to wash everything to get rid of the smell.

Big chunks of wood burned fiercely, throwing their heat into the room and making me feel a little better. The house was big and comfortable and warm. Thick rugs covered the floor. The sofas and chairs were the kind you could sink into, and lots of interesting pictures hung on the log walls. Through the open door of another room I could see the usual electronic equipment—television, stereo, computer—but there was no sign of the elaborate security devices that the Einsteins said had tracked our movements from the moment we ditched our bikes beside the Kispiox Road.

In answer to their questions we'd admitted our suspicions about the raven mask. They didn't seem bothered to be taken for thieves. Instead I got the feeling they'd wanted us to investigate so they could test their security system.

Even so, Dawn apologized several times for our raid. "My parents will be really annoyed," she said. "It was a stupid thing to do."

"Don't worry about it," Ma Einstein said. "Maybe we won't even tell them."

"Why do you have such fancy security?" I asked. "Most people around here don't even lock their doors, and Dad's church is always open. Yet you go to all this trouble to protect your place."

"We've got some valuable things here."

"Do you mean those pictures on the wall?"

"I painted those. No, our treasures of the Gitksan are upstairs. They're worth a lot of money."

"May we see them?"

For a moment she stared at me. Then she looked at her husband. "How about some food for these kids? I imagine they're hungry."

"Coming up," he said, disappearing into the kitchen.

As I listened to the rattle of pots and pans, I thought about the Einsteins' treasures upstairs. Why didn't they just let me see them, if they had nothing to hide? What if the raven mask was up there? I tried to figure out a way to sneak up and get a look. It had been humiliating to drop into the slime pit but at least it had got us into the house. If I could catch a glimpse of the mask, and then tell the police, it would make up for everything.

Pa Einstein's head appeared around the corner. "How hungry are you two?"

Dawn smiled. "Just a cup of tea, thanks."

"I could eat a horse," I said.

"How about some boiled moose nose?"

I studied his face, trying to decide if he was joking. Then I glanced at Dawn, hoping she'd give me a wink or something, but she ignored me.

"I . . . uh . . . I'm . . ."

"Not up to it?" Pa Einstein shook his head. "Kids these days don't appreciate good food. Okay, then, how about some smoked bear intestines? They've got a nice fatty taste. You'll love them."

Something heaved inside me. Sweat broke out on my forehead and again I looked at Dawn for help. But she was in another world, and Ma Einstein's face revealed nothing. Then she leaned forward, opening a jar from a side table.

"This is *sa xulgwa*. Try it, you'll like it."

Were they trying to poison me because I'd guessed the truth about the mask? I hesitated, then realized I was being stupid. I took a crisp green leaf from the jar and had a small bite. It was salty, but tasted good.

"That's seaweed," Ma Einstein said. "Good, eh?"

"Did your husband really mean it about the moose nose?"

"He was teasing, but in the old days our people ate all parts of an animal. There were no supermarkets then, so we relied on nature. We took only what we needed, and used as much of it as we could. Intestines, eyes, ears. I remember as a little girl eating beaver tail, nice and crisp out of the fire. Anything that couldn't be used was buried, to show our respect for the animal."

Pa Einstein appeared carrying mugs of tea and a plate of food for me. The tea was hot and sweet, and I quickly worked my way through slabs of homemade bread and some delicious eggs that were a rich yellow colour.

"Those are from our henhouse," he said. "You won't get eggs like that in a supermarket."

"They're fantastic. Better than my dad's cooking."

"We've met your father. He's a minister, right?"

"Yes."

"I wonder how he feels about what the missionaries did to our people."

"What do you mean?"

"When the Europeans first arrived on the Pacific coast they were welcomed. But they brought alcohol, and diseases like measles and smallpox. Thousands of our people died. The missionaries wouldn't let us pray in our own language and they burned many totem poles."

"But why?"

"They saw the animals on the poles and believed we were worshipping something evil. They banned our great feasts, what some call the potlatch, and destroyed our culture. The Europeans thought we'd become a part of their culture if ours was dead."

Ma Einstein leaned toward me. "We Gitksan people were fortunate. On the coast most of the Native traditions were destroyed but we lived far inland, away from missionaries and other Europeans. So our culture has remained strong to this day. But it still needs protecting."

Her husband nodded. "That's why we collect Gitksan treasures. They should be here, not in museums in Texas and Tokyo."

So the Einsteins were collectors. I looked at them, remembering how Grace had been afraid that the raven mask would fall into the hands of a collector. More and more the finger of guilt was pointing at the Einsteins, but what I needed was some proof.

"Where are your treasures? Why can't I see them?"

Pa Einstein looked at me with solemn eyes. "You still think we've got the raven mask, don't you?"

"I, um . . ."

"You should trust us, young man. Our word is our bond. We collect modern treasures, carved by people like Dawn's brother Ezra. What you saw in the back seat of our car was a raven mask made for us by Ezra."

"Then why can't I see your treasures?"

"Because I don't believe you're genuinely interested in art. You're just after the raven mask, and you don't trust us. There aren't many people who truly appreciate our culture. Most see our artifacts as exotic things to gawk at or possess. Your mother was one of the few people who really understood the Gitksan."

I looked at him in surprise. "You knew her?"

"Of course. She sat in the very chair you're sitting in, the day she came to see our treasures. Her questions were thoughtful because she was sincerely interested."

"Are you saying I'm not?" When he didn't reply I pressed the point. "You don't trust me, do you?"

"Nobody's saying that, Graham, but you must admit it's difficult to trust someone who's just attempted a break-in."

"I've apologized for that, but all you've done since then is pick on me. You say I don't appreciate your culture, and you even made rude remarks about Dad being a minister. He doesn't go around burning down totem poles, you know."

"Hey, calm down." Pa Einstein raised a hand. "Nobody's accused you or your father of anything. Just relax. . ."

Dawn looked at me. "He's right, Graham. Knock it off. You're sounding dumb."

For a moment I watched the flames leaping in the fireplace. Then I stood up. "Do you think my clothes are dry yet? I feel like going home."

When Ma Einstein returned with my clothes I thanked her, then carried them to the bathroom where I'd had my shower. It had been a lousy evening so far, but things weren't over yet. If I could somehow find the mask before we left the house, my fall into the slime pit would be forgotten and Dawn wouldn't be so disgusted with me.

It would be risky, but I had to try.

As I stepped into the hallway I heard voices from the living-room. I paused, making sure I could hear both Pa and Ma Einstein, then looked at a nearby staircase. It led up into darkness. Taking a deep breath, I started up. Fortunately there were no squeaks from the wood as I climbed. Reaching a landing, I hesitated before forcing myself to continue climbing. Then, when I got to the upper hallway, I couldn't believe my eyes.

Through an open door I saw the raven mask.

It hung on the wall surrounded by others like Bear and Eagle and Wolf. Small spotlights glowed from the ceiling, picking out the rich colours of each mask. I stared at them, not really believing my eyes. So I tiptoed along the hallway to the door of the room.

The raven looked exactly like the one stolen from Dawn. Even the wood seemed old. Deciding I had to get closer, I entered the room.

A siren howled.

I stopped dead, horrified by the noise. Desperately I looked around for the siren. The noise was deafening. Then it suddenly stopped as the Einsteins and Dawn appeared beside me.

"I'm sorry," I said. "Believe me, I feel terrible."

Nobody said anything. They all just stared at me with their sad, dark eyes.

* * *

I guess my friendship with Dawn hit rock-bottom after that. She was furious and embarrassed because I'd made such an idiot of myself at the Einsteins, and I couldn't say I really blamed her. The next day I went by her house to apologize—and also to find out from Ezra if he'd really made the raven mask at the Einsteins—but neither was home.

A neighbour told me Dawn had gone to her dance

rehearsal, so I rode to 'Ksan on my bike. Because of the sunny weather the dancers were going to rehearse on the grass in front of the communal houses. The tall trees of the forest threw long shadows across the group of dancers who talked together while waiting for Grace to arrive. I searched for Dawn's face, then saw her sitting alone in front of one of the houses.

"Hi," I said, walking over. "Listen, Dawn . . . I'm really sorry about last night. I guess I should have listened to you about the Einsteins."

She shook her head. "I'm sorry I was mad at you. I know you were just trying to help find the mask."

For a while we sat quietly, then I turned to her. "I'm glad you turned up for the rehearsal."

"Yeah." She looked across the sunny lawn at the other dancers. "But I don't really know why I'm here. I don't want to dance."

"How come?"

"It doesn't seem important anymore."

I stared at her. "What garbage. How many times have you talked about your dancing being your whole life? Now you're saying it doesn't matter?"

"I used to dance because I wanted to . . . to express my love for my people. I know that probably sounds stupid, but . . ."

"Dawn, what's the matter with you? Don't let a few gossips get you down."

"Why should I care anymore when . . ."

"Look, I'm getting sick of this stuff. You just hang around feeling sorry for yourself. Where's your pride? You should get out there and dance like never before! Show them what you're made of."

She shifted uneasily. "Forget it."

"Okay, suit yourself." I stood up. As I walked away I hoped Dawn would follow but she didn't.

I found a place on the grass beside a girl from school. Like me, she wasn't a Gitksan, but I often saw her here.

"Hi," she said. "I'm surprised you're still hanging out with Dawn."

"What do you mean, Susan?"

"Well, I mean, everyone knows she stole the mask."

I stared at her. "I thought you two were friends. Now you've dropped her because of a bunch of lies?"

"Who says they're lies?"

I kicked at the ground with my boot. "I figure a true friend is someone who stands by you when other people have turned their backs."

"You're just saying that because you've got a crush on Dawn. It's so obvious."

"How I feel about Dawn doesn't make any difference. I'd stand up for anyone, even you. And I sure don't have a crush on you."

Moving away from Susan, I sprawled on the grass by myself. As I did, Grace picked up a skin-covered drum. "Okay," she said to the dancers, "let's start with the Feast of the Animals. The young children enter first, then the older group." As she thumped on the drum, each dancer crossed the grass, acting the part of a forest animal. Some were difficult to recognize, others quite easy. My favourite was Grace's own daughter, a tiny girl of four who was Frog. She crouched with her tongue darting in and out, then sprang forward in great leaps. The older dancers grinned at her, then watched carefully as Grace demonstrated how to make their arms move like bird wings or how to make pecking motions with their heads.

"Remember," she said, "once you're all assembled on stage you hear the approach of We'gyet. You're supposed to look worried. Then We'gyet enters and blows you away. Act like you're being swept off the stage by a powerful wind. Don't wander away like you're going somewhere to watch TV, for crying out loud!"

The dancers laughed, then some girls wrapped themselves in scarlet button-blankets. They were hand-sewn with as many as two thousand mother-of-pearl buttons that showed crests of animals like Frog and Killer Whale.

The girls spread their blankets to form a shield. As Grace pounded the drum they began to sway, then moved aside to reveal Grouse. I understood a bit of this legend because Grouse was danced by a friend of mine named Tom. As he danced, with his hands making fluttering motions, I listened for the drum to sound the *CRACK!* of a gunshot. When it did, Tom fell to his knees. I held my breath, watching the agony of the wounded grouse, then relaxed when it managed to escape from the hunter.

When the dance ended Tom went over to speak to Grace. She nodded, then he suddenly walked straight across the grass to Dawn. Kneeling down in front of her he spoke to her quietly and then held out his hand. She hesitated, then let Tom pull her to her feet. As they came close toward us I could see Dawn's eyes searching the faces of the other dancers.

One of the girls went forward and linked her arm

through Dawn's. Then others went up and suddenly she was surrounded by smiling faces. Grace gently tapped on the drum as she grinned at Dawn.

"Okay, lazybones. You've missed two rehearsals, so let's see some work."

Dawn looked at the other dancers. Her face was glowing. As she started her dance she seemed hesitant, but then her emotions took over. Faster and faster she moved until her feet were a blur, flying in time to the pounding rhythm of the drum. The moment the dance finished everyone crowded around with congratulations, and even the ravens in the trees seemed to join in with raucous cries.

"Okay," Grace said, "let's wrap up rehearsal with the Spirit Ball."

The dancers always enjoyed this one, and today they really got into it. The idea was they threw a large, imaginary ball around a circle and each person who received it had to perform a short dance. Those watching had to imitate each motion the dancer made. The skill lay in following the rapidly changing motions, and there was usually a lot of laughter as people were tricked into making false moves.

When the rehearsal ended, the dancers took off their button-blankets and other regalia, and suddenly they were just ordinary kids wearing Nikes and jeans and Montreal Expos T-shirts.

"Hey, you kids," Grace said, as people got on their bikes. "Don't forget we're dancing for VIPs on Friday. A bunch of Japanese and German tourists, so no gum-chewing on stage. Let's show them Canadians have style!"

"Trust us," someone said, and the dancers laughed as they rode away. Grace was popular with her dancers, and I felt good as I watched her hug Dawn goodbye.

"So," I said, as she joined me, "how about heading to the B.C. for milkshakes?"

"Sure, but first I've got to get a message to Ezra." As we started walking toward the House of Carvers she looked at me. "My parents phoned this morning. I managed to avoid mentioning the mask, but they'll be home the day after tomorrow. I'm going to be in deep trouble, Graham."

"Then maybe we'd better run away together."

She laughed. "You're as bad as Connor Gentry."

"Old nicotine breath? Come on, give me a break."

A boom box was playing loud music as we went inside the House of Carvers. Ezra sat at his workbench staring bleakly at the carving he was working on. As Dawn walked over to him Connor Gentry came in and sat down at a nearby bench. He leaned over his work and I realized this was my chance to ask him some questions about the stove at the rodeo grounds.

Walking over, I managed a smile. "Hi, how's it going?"

"Okay." He didn't even look up.

"Hey, that's some motorcycle you've got. I bet it was expensive."

"You're right about that. I'm still paying off the bank loan."

"Ever ride out to the Kispiox Valley?"

"Lots of times. Why?"

"I don't know. I just . . ."

Connor's black eyes cut into me and suddenly I was afraid. My face burned, and I tried desperately to change the subject.

"Where, um . . . what's that you're working on?"

"A bent box." He picked up a long piece of wood. "This is grooved in three places. After the wood's steamed to make the grooves soft, it's bent to form a square. The ends are pegged together, then the box is fitted with a top and bottom."

"What are they used for?"

"Cooking, or storing possessions." He pointed at the design on the box. "This tells the legend of how Raven the Trickster stole the daylight and kept it in a bent box."

"What are you going to do with it when it's finished?"

He laughed. "What do you think? Find a buyer, of course. I need the money."

He returned to his work and I realized I'd blown my feeble attempt at being a detective. Slowly I walked toward Ezra's bench, thinking of all the questions I should have asked.

Ezra gave me a tired smile. "How're you doing?"

"Okay, I guess." I looked at the mask of Bear on the workbench. Its staring eyes and jagged teeth were magnificent. "Will you sell this one to the Einsteins?"

"Maybe."

"So it's true that they buy your stuff?"

"Of course."

"Including a raven mask?"

He nodded. "They're good collectors. I appreciate their desire to keep our art close by."

"Do carvers make a lot of money?"

"We do okay." Smiling, Ezra glanced across the room at Connor Gentry. "But some of us have major ambitions. Want to know what's big in Connor's life right now? At coffee this morning he talked about buying a condo in Hawaii. The rest of us think he's dreaming in Technicolor, but he sounds pretty determined."

I looked at Connor, then turned to Dawn. "Condos cost a fortune," I whispered. *"Where's he getting the money?"*

8

I kept thinking about Connor as we sat over milkshakes at the café. Dawn wasn't interested in my theories and soon left to visit her grandmother. For a while I brooded alone. Then I went outside.

Grabbing my bike, I headed for 'Ksan, thinking I'd try again to ask Connor some questions. As I rode into the parking lot I saw him sitting on his motorcycle talking to Dark-Sky Thunder. Connor was waving a hand in the air and his face looked angrier than usual. Then he suddenly gunned the motorcycle and took off, spraying dust and pebbles in all directions.

Dark-Sky Thunder watched him go, then disappeared into the grounds of 'Ksan. Probably a great detective would have followed, but I wasn't feeling too great so I decided to head home. Then, as I rode past the school, I saw a police car stopped ahead with its lights flashing. In front of it was the car of my dreams. Ray West avoided my eyes as I slowly pedalled past, trying to see what was happening. The Mountie seemed to be writing a speeding ticket, but for a while after I couldn't help wondering if she'd stopped Ray as part of the search for the missing mask.

* * *

I saw the crying woman a few hours later.

She stood in an open field with wooden tears falling from her eyes. "That's really something," I said, getting out of Ezra's car. "Was she carved from a single tree?"

"Yup."

We walked with Dawn through the tall grass toward the pole. "What does it mean? Why is she crying?"

"Totem poles have different purposes. Some give the history of the family, telling us the village it first came from, the problems the family has overcome and the territory for which it's responsible." He looked at the crying woman. "Other poles record a single event that happened long ago."

"So, what happened to her?"

"I can't tell you. That story belongs only to the chief of the clan. It's private, just like many legends and dances." When I looked disappointed, he went on. "But let me tell you a different legend. Some of our totems warn against abusing nature. In one village the children tormented fish in the river. When thunder rumbled across the sky the elders told the children it was a warning to stop, but they just laughed and said the sky was noisy because the spirits had empty stomachs. The the earth opened and the entire village was destroyed."

I looked at the totems, wondering if I could spot that legend. On one pole I could see unhappy-looking children holding their stomachs, but no designs that looked like fish.

The totems stood in two long rows with the distant mountains beyond. Nearby were the houses and churches of Kispiox, and the surging waters of the two rivers that met at the village. We were there because Ezra and Dawn had invited me to attend a death feast.

"Tell me again what's going to happen tonight?" I asked.

"The chief of the Wolf Clan just lost his brother in a boating accident. The funeral was earlier today, and now we're going to a ceremony called a death feast. When we get there you'll understand more."

"It may last all night," Dawn warned.

"You're joking."

"You won't be able to get up from your place, either, because that's disrespectful to the host chief. Once you're seated you stay until the end."

On our way through Kispiox we passed comfortable-looking homes and a school with Native crests painted on the walls. As we approached the community hall Ezra handed me a bowl and spoon. "Each guest brings these. In ancient times they'd have been beautifully carved from wood."

All kinds of people were arriving for the death feast. I said hello to some kids from school as we entered the hall, then started toward a table. But Ezra grabbed my arm.

"Wait, Graham. We have to be seated by the chief."

He pointed at a man who was surprisingly young, with thick black hair and a handsome face. He escorted an old man to one of the many tables arranged around the hall, then another person to a different table.

"There's a special place for the chief of each clan to sit," Dawn said. "Everyone else is seated according to their position in the clan."

"There are hundreds of people here. How does that man remember where everyone sits?"

"He's got a good mind. That's why he's a chief."

"Where will I be? I don't belong to any clan."

"He'll probably put you with us."

Eventually it was our turn. The chief gave me a friendly handshake, then led us past the many tables. I looked at some crests on the wall, then noticed an electronic basketball scoreboard.

"Tonight the hall is recognized as the young chief's feast house," Ezra explained.

As we sat down beside the Einsteins they grinned. "We watched your video last night, Graham. An Oscar-winning performance."

Pretending not to hear, I ignored them. For a long time the hall continued to fill with people, including Dad and Virginia, and there was the constant noise of voices. Then an old man stood up and people fell silent.

His voice was soft, and I couldn't understand what he said, but at the end everyone said "Amen." Then people began to move among the tables with steaming containers of soup. The moment my bowl was filled I dug in, then ate several pieces of fried bread. Soon I leaned back feeling pleasantly full. Right away a beaming woman appeared with the soup container and refilled my bowl.

As she walked away, Pa Einstein laughed. "Never been to a feast before?"

I shook my head.

"Your bowl will never be empty."

"But I can't keep eating forever."

"Then leave food in your bowl, and carry it home after the feast. We call such extra food *so'o*. In the old days the chiefs took home enough *so'o* to feed all members of the family. We have never wasted what the Great Nature provides."

I tried to picture a Wolf Clan communal house a thousand years ago. It was hard to believe that feasts had begun so long ago and continued to this day, and that I was witnessing such an ancient ceremony. I looked around the hall, envying the traditions that bound these people so closely together. Some people were laughing. Others were quietly talking and some cried openly about the loss of the chief's brother. I was a bit shocked that people would laugh at a death feast, but then I remembered Dawn telling me that her people both laughed and cried as they remembered those who had died.

Ma Einstein looked at me. "I'll tell you what our people say: walk softly on, for this is the breath of our forefathers."

"I don't understand."

"Within me is the breath of my grandparents, and one day my breath will be found within the children of my grandchildren. So your mother lives on inside you."

Her husband nodded. "Your actions tell the world how you feel about your mother. If you are strong and proud, you honour her. If you help others, if you smile at a stranger, you are showing them your mother's love."

"That's really beautiful. Thank you for telling me."

"We knew your mother," Ma Einstein said. "We can see within you her strength and goodness."

For a long time I sat thinking about Mom. For the first time, remembering her didn't make me feel sad.

"This has been a really special evening for me," I finally said to Ezra. "Thanks for inviting me."

"It's not over yet. There's still the passing of the dead man's name."

As he said this a man stood up. In a high, thin voice he sang for a long time. When he'd finished, Ezra leaned close to me. "That was a mourning song. It told how the dead man's name came to be, back in the days when our people formed their first village. It is said the village was so big that if a flock of birds flew over they would die of exhaustion before reaching the last house." He paused as a girl walked toward the chief, who spoke to her in the Gitksan language. "She's receiving her dead uncle's name. It's a cherished possession, given only to those who have earned it. She is now worthy to sit in the feast house."

Dawn looked at me. "She'll arrange for a totem or tombstone and then build a fence around her uncle's grave."

"Why a fence?"

"It's a good way to work out her grief."

I was going to ask more when a man at our table stood up. For a long time he spoke in the Gitksan language, then sat down. Another man began to speak, followed by someone else.

"Each of them is a chief," Ezra whispered. "They are acknowledging the truth of what was said by the younger chief. The girl is being told her responsibilities. Acquiring a high-ranking name means she will help strengthen the Wolf. The chiefs are also thanking the Wolf Clan for their hospitality."

By the time the death feast ended I was feeling pretty wiped out. Ezra and Dad stayed behind to help with the clean-up, but Virginia offered Dawn and me a ride home. As we went outside into the cold air I looked at my watch. It was after two in the morning.

But when I got home I didn't go to bed. I was full of all the things that had happened over the past few days, and I wanted to get it all down while it was still fresh in my mind. I sat at my computer thinking about the death feast and the dance rehearsal and Dawn's feelings about her people. Then, as I started working, the phone rang. When I picked it up I hardly recognized Dawn's voice.

"Graham," she cried. "You've got to help me!"

9

The hair on my neck stood up. That's how scared I felt when I heard Dawn's voice.

"What is it? What's wrong?"

"The graveyard . . . the mask, it's . . ."

"Dawn, calm down. What's happened?"

I heard her take a deep breath. Then she said, "The mask is hidden in the cemetery! I'm going up there."

"Now?" I looked at my watch. "It's after three and pitch-black out. Why not wait until morning?"

"The man said to go now."

"What man? Dawn, what's this all about?"

"Right after I got home the phone rang. I thought Ezra was calling, but it was some man. His voice was muffled, like he'd disguised it. I couldn't tell who was calling."

"What did he say?"

"That the mask is hidden in a gravehouse. I'm going up to the cemetery, Graham, and . . ."

"Hold it, Dawn. This doesn't make sense. Why should someone call you at three in the morning with this kind of story?"

"I don't know and I don't care! It's a real chance to find the mask."

I shook my head. "Something weird's going on. I wish Dad was home. He'd know what to do."

"I'm going up there, Graham."

"Not without me. I'll meet you at the path to the cemetery."

I hurried downstairs. King left his box beside the stove and trotted over to me, looking sleepy. He wasn't the world's bravest dog, but it would be good having him along. Just in case.

The air outside was cold and clear. The moonlight was intense, throwing long shadows across the yard as King and I hurried past the church, cut through a yard and soon reached the path leading up to the graveyard.

There was no sign of Dawn. I shivered, then knelt to hug King. "It's okay, boy," I whispered. "She'll be coming soon." As he licked my face I looked at the nearby houses. No lights showed. It was as if I was the only person in the world.

Something moved in the darkness. My heart leapt, then I recognized Dawn. She had come out of nowhere, making so little noise that even King hadn't noticed her approach.

"Are you okay?" I asked.

She nodded, but her voice shook a little. "I'm glad you brought King."

"Are you sure you want to do this?"

"Yes. I've got to."

"Then let's get it over with."

Together we climbed the path. Neither of us said a word. Soon we reached the graveyard on the bench of land overlooking Hazelton. The leaves of the trees and bushes looked silver in the moonlight, and so did the old tombstones. I looked in the direction of my mother's grave.

"Where are we supposed to find the mask?" I asked.

"In the gravehouse of a chief of my clan."

"Is it around here?"

Dawn shook her head. "It's on the far side of the graveyard."

I swallowed. "This isn't much fun."

"I know. But we've got to try."

We started walking. Never before had I noticed the number of hiding places here. Anyone could have been inside a gravehouse, watching us pass by, or hidden behind the bushes that grew everywhere. An owl hooted, and the wind rustled the leaves. The massive shape of Stek'yaw'den rose above us into a sky that was littered with stars.

"Wait!" Dawn gripped my arm. "Why is King growling?"

I looked down. King stood with legs planted, staring ahead into the darkness. A growl sounded from deep in his throat. "He hardly ever does that. There's something wrong."

We both peered into the darkness, looking for strange

movements in the shadows. Then Dawn shook her head. "Probably it's just some night creature bothering him. Come on, Graham."

The next few minutes were the longest of my life, but eventually we reached the gravehouse. It was very old and leaned to one side, creaking in the wind. The door was open; I could see nothing inside but darkness.

"Where's the mask supposed to be?" I whispered.

"I don't know. Maybe in the rafters. We'll have to look."

"Didn't you bring a flashlight?"

"No. I didn't think of it."

"I hope the mask's not buried. I'm not digging up a grave."

My mouth was dry. King continued to growl as I stared at the gravehouse. We moved forward to the door and stepped inside. The gravehouse was so dark I could hardly see anything. I was turning to speak to Dawn when I heard the door creak. Then King began to bark furiously.

"Ssssh," I said, kneeling down beside him. "You're scaring me half to death."

The dim shape of Dawn moved around the walls as she explored the gravehouse. "This place is empty," she said. "The mask isn't here."

"Are you sure this is the right gravehouse?"

"Yes."

"Then maybe . . ." I paused. "What was that?"

"I didn't hear anything."

"There was some kind of sound, like a . . ." Again I paused. "There it is again! It's like something tapping on the roof."

"Let's get out of here." Dawn tried the door, then whirled around. "It won't open!"

"You're kidding." Quickly I went to the door and pushed. "It's locked or something."

"Listen!" Dawn looked up at the roof. The sounds were clear now—a *ping* followed by silence, then another *ping*. "It's just like when Alicia's father died," she whispered. "During the funeral everyone heard rain on the church roof, but it was a clear night. The elders said his spirit was lingering."

I pushed the door with all my strength, but it wouldn't move. King was barking like crazy.

"We shouldn't have come here. That phone call was setting us up."

"But why?"

"Because we've been trying to find the mask. I wish we'd . . ."

"Graham, I smell smoke."

Dawn stepped closer to me, and I could see that her eyes were huge. Then I saw something moving. It was smoke, seeping through a crack in the wall.

"Oh, no," Dawn moaned. "We're going to die, and it's all my fault."

Quickly I pulled off my jacket and stuffed it into the crack. That stopped the smoke, but within seconds it started coming through another crack. My eyes began to sting. Then I was coughing.

Dawn dropped to the ground. "Get down here. The smoke's thinner."

I fell to my knees and crawled toward the door. Gathering all my strength I pushed with both my hands. The door flew open. King ran into the open air and I crawled after him with Dawn at my side. For a few seconds we lay there, coughing and spluttering. Then I staggered to my feet.

"Come on, let's get out of here!"

As King barked beside us we staggered through the graveyard, still coughing. Finally we reached the path and stumbled down toward town. When we reached the yard of a house near the church Dawn turned to me.

"We could have died!"

"We've got to tell the Mounties." I knelt down to calm King. Suddenly I stared at the church. "Dawn! Did you see that?"

"See what?"

"Look at the church! There's a light in the tower. I'm sure of it."

Keeping my eyes on the tower, I walked toward the church. The moonlight threw deep shadows across the yard behind the building, making it difficult to see the path.

"There's the light again!" I grabbed Dawn's arm.

"Yes, I see it. Maybe your dad's in the tower."

"At four in the morning? Come on, let's find out what's going on."

As I hurried through the shadows toward the church my foot connected with a metal trash can and knocked it over. When the lid hit the path it made a racket that filled the night. I grabbed at the lid, trying to keep it quiet, then looked again at the church tower.

The light had gone out.

"Let's hurry!"

King began barking as we ran forward. I tried to shush him, but that only got him more excited. By the time we pulled open the door King's barking had announced our arrival, so we didn't worry about making a lot of noise as we ran through the church to the bell tower.

Flicking on a light, I looked up at the ceiling where a wooden ladder led to an open trap door. "That thing's always closed! Dad is really fussy about it."

Dawn gazed into the darkness beyond the trap door. "What's up there?"

"I don't know for sure." I tried to smile. "I'm not crazy about heights, so I've never actually climbed the ladder. Dad says there's a little room where the Boys Brigade meets during the winter, and another ladder that leads up to the tower rafters where the bell hangs."

"How does it get rung?"

I pointed to a rope hanging from the ceiling. "Someone pulls that."

Dawn walked over to the ladder. "I'm going up there."

"Do you . . . uh . . . do you want help?"

She shook her head. "You and King stand guard down here."

"Good idea." I looked at her, feeling both embarrassed and anxious. "Be careful."

Quickly she climbed the ladder and disappeared through the trap door. I heard her feet moving around above me. Then yellow light streamed down through the opening. "I found the light switch," Dawn called. "It's pretty nice up here. The brigade's got their banners on the wall and . . . hey!"

"What is it?" But Dawn didn't answer. "Are you okay?"

There was no reply. I paced the floor and called to Dawn again. When she still didn't answer I knew I *had* to climb the ladder. As I started toward it, Dawn appeared above me.

In her hands was the raven mask.

"I don't believe it." I stared at the mask. "Where . . ."

Dawn was grinning so hard I thought her face would split apart. Holding the mask under one arm, she came quickly down the ladder and then did a victory dance while King barked and I laughed with joy and relief.

"I don't believe it," I kept saying. "I just don't believe it!"

Finally Dawn put the mask on a small table and hugged me. Her eyes glistened. "It's over, Graham. We found it!"

"But where did you find it?"

"The floor of the meeting room is really dusty. I could see footprints leading to one corner, where someone had dropped a few burnt matches. They must have made the light you saw in the tower. Anyway, I decided the person must have been up there looking for something, then was scared away by all the noise we made. So I checked out the wall."

"And you found a secret panel?"

"Sort of, I guess." She grinned. "The wall is panelled with wood. I could see there was a small cupboard in the corner. The handle was missing, but I managed to work the door open using a nail I found on the floor."

"And the mask was inside?"

"When I opened the door I couldn't see anything.

The cupboard was bare, just like in the nursery rhyme. But I figured there had to be something in there, so I crawled inside to take a look. Above my head was a hollow. Inside was the mask."

"Congratulations." I smiled at her. "You know something? I was right to say we needed faith. Who'd have thought the mask was hidden inside Dad's church all along?"

"But who put it here?"

"Maybe the crook left some fingerprints." We both looked at the mask. "We'd better phone the police."

Dawn picked up the mask. "At last I can stand tall again in this town."

At that moment King began growling. I looked down at him and followed his gaze in the direction of the church sanctuary. It was in darkness, but I could see a few wooden pews gleaming in the light coming from behind us.

"What is it?" I bent down beside King, feeling the stiff hackles on his neck. "Dawn," I said slowly. "Something's wrong."

Again I looked into the darkness of the sanctuary, and this time I found out why King was growling. Out of the shadows came Bear, holding the gun.

10

I grabbed King.

I knew if he tried to attack Bear, he'd be shot. Pulling him close, I stared at the fierce mask with its staring eyes and sharp teeth.

The person inside the bear regalia moved closer, gesturing at the mask with his gun. I could sense Dawn's hesitation, but then she handed it over. Without a word Bear turned and ran through the darkened sanctuary.

King tried desperately to escape from my arms, but I held tight. Mask or no mask, he was too precious to lose. Looking up at Dawn, I saw tears running down her cheeks. "I'm really sorry," I said. "It's just not fair."

"I give up." Dawn wiped her eyes, then slumped

down in the nearest pew. "I just don't care anymore."

Letting go of King, I grabbed the rope hanging from the ceiling. As I pulled on it I heard the deep gonging of the bell high above. "We've got to get help. Bear might try to hide somewhere near the church."

"It's no use, Graham. Forget it."

"No way."

I tried to concentrate my attention on the bell, but I was really just thinking about Dawn. It seemed impossible that she could have held the mask in her hands and then lost it again. How had Bear known? He must have been the person in the tower who'd been scared off by our noise. Maybe he'd been hiding in the sanctuary the whole time, listening to every word we said.

Suddenly the door beside me was thrown open. I was overcome with relief when I saw Dad.

As quickly as possible we told him the story, then had to repeat it as other people came in the door, alerted by the clanging of the bell. Dad switched on the sanctuary lights as we talked to the organist, who'd been the first to arrive, followed by Connor Gentry, Ezra, Virginia, Ray, Grace and others. Ezra kept one arm around Dawn as he listened to our story. Then he shook his head.

"It could have been much worse. That fool might have shot you. Dawn, you've got to stop this crazy detective work."

"But I found the mask! I had it in my hands, Ezra. We were just about to phone the police."

"You're sure it was the original transformation mask?"

"Yes! When I found it, I couldn't believe my eyes."

"And it was in the tower?"

Dawn nodded. "In the room where your brigade meets."

"Tell me again about the graveyard."

Once more Dawn described the mysterious phone call that had lured us to the cemetery, then the terrible moment when we'd smelled smoke. "We could have been killed, Ezra."

He nodded. "You're right, and that's why you should have stayed home. If anything had happened tonight, I'd never have forgiven myself."

I looked at the people sitting in the church, trying to read their faces. Connor Gentry looked angry, which was nothing new, but most of the others just seemed tired, and I couldn't tell what was going through their minds.

Then a terrible thought struck me. What if one of them was secretly Bear?

* * *

Little of the night remained by the time I got to bed. I tossed and turned, unable to forget the image of Bear appearing suddenly in the darkened church.

Eventually I dragged myself out of bed and had some breakfast. With King beside me I went to the store for some almonds, then sat on the church steps eating them. The air was cold and crisp, carrying the first hint of autumn. Ragged clouds blew across the sky and a wind stirred the leaves of the trees.

Dawn came along the street shortly after and joined me on the steps. "Connor came by my place this morning."

"After you again, I suppose."

"No, listen. He told me that Dark-Sky Thunder's been camped on his land but he left yesterday."

"Why?"

"Connor kicked him off. He said he was worried Dark-Sky Thunder would break into his house and steal something, but I got the feeling he mostly wanted that guy out of his life."

"So Dark-Sky Thunder's headed back to the prairies?"

She shook her head. "Connor figures he's gone up to January Village."

"The old ghost town overlooking the canyon? Why's he gone there?"

"Well, there are a couple of old canoes he could use to fish, and I guess he could live in one of the buildings. But what I can't understand is why he's still hanging around this area. The rodeo ended days ago."

"Something to do with the mask, I bet."

"Could be." Dawn sighed. "My parents arrive home tomorrow. Fat lot we can do to get the mask back before then."

"Why don't we check out that gravehouse?"

"Are you nuts?"

"Come on. It won't seem so scary in the daylight. We can search the remains and maybe figure out what caused the fire."

As we walked through the cemetery I kept looking over my shoulder. I don't know what I expected, but my eyes searched every possible hiding place. Then we got a real shock.

"The gravehouse," Dawn exclaimed. "It's still standing!"

"But there was all that smoke. I'd swear it burnt to a crisp."

We hurried forward, looking for signs of damage but finding nothing. "That's impossible," I said. "The wood should be charred, at least."

Dawn shivered. "Ghosts did it."

I smiled. "Get serious, Dawn. Do ghosts wear cowboy boots?"

"What do you mean?"

I pointed at the soft ground. "Those marks were made by cowboy boots, and they look fresh to me."

"You're wearing cowboy boots."

I put my foot inside a mark. "That boot's much larger than mine. Some huge guy's been here recently."

"Dark-Sky Thunder."

I nodded. "Do you think he was at the church, too?"

"No. He's too tall for that bear regalia."

"I still bet Dark-Sky Thunder's involved in all this." I looked at Dawn. "I guess you know what we should do."

"Ride our bikes to January Village?"

I nodded.

"But shouldn't we phone the police?"

"What'll we say? That Dark-Sky Thunder used to live in a field near Connor and now he may be living at January Village? So what?"

"Then why should *we* go out there?"

"Because your parents arrive home tomorrow, and because everybody else seems to have forgotten about the mask. The Mounties sure haven't found it."

"Maybe we should tell Ezra."

"Forget it. He doesn't like us playing detective, remember?"

Dawn was quiet for a moment. Then she said, "Okay, Graham, let's head out there."

Before long we were riding along the dirt road that led in the direction of the ghost town. The many potholes rattled my teeth, and the forest grew so thick that we were getting scratched by the branches that dangled over the road. To make things worse, the sky had darkened and the air was cold and damp, threatening rain. I was glad we'd decided to leave King at home. He'd have been miserable by now.

Eventually we hid our bikes in the forest and followed a path through the trees until we reached a clearing and saw the remains of a collapsed building.

"That looks like a house."

"It probably used to be one."

"How depressing."

Only one wall remained standing, punched by an empty hole where a window had been. The wood was grey, the floor scattered with broken glass. Trees grew up where the rooms used to be, and I knew that before long there'd be nothing here except the forest.

"I wonder who lived here. Was this a Native village?"

Dawn shook her head. "About fifty years ago some settlers came up here from the United States. They built homes and a school and a community hall, but I guess the wilderness was too much for them. The families eventually all left."

"There's no one here now?"

"Nope. The last family left years ago. Since then a few people have fixed up some of the houses or built cabins, but nobody has lasted. It's just too lonely a place."

I looked at the huge trees all around and the dark shadows of the forest. "Anyone could be watching us," I said quietly. "Maybe we should go back."

"Not before we look around. That's why we came here."

Moving past the wrecked house we looked up at the cold sky. I shivered, wishing I'd brought warmer clothes, then pointed across the clearing. "I think that's the old school."

"You're right. Want to have a look?"

"I guess so."

The remains of a swing dangled from a tree outside the school. It was a small building with a peaked roof and walls that sagged inwards, close to collapsing. The front door had fallen off and lay among the bushes nearby. We climbed the steps of a small porch and tiptoed inside.

"What a place to study," I whispered, looking at the small room with its low ceiling. The wind blew through the empty windows, lifting and swirling scraps of paper on the floor. Only a single desk remained. "Here's an old geography book," I said, looking inside. "It's covered with mildew."

"I found some chalk."

The wind was cold. I blew on my hands, then put them in my pockets as Dawn gingerly climbed some wooden stairs to the next floor. "Nothing much to see," she called. "I think the teacher lived up here."

I went to the window and looked at the dark forest. Then we left the school and followed a path past the remains of several collapsed houses and through the forest to another clearing.

"What's that?" I pointed at a flimsy wooden structure in the distance.

"It looks like a wrecked bridge."

As we approached the bridge I realized we were above a river canyon. The old structure had once connected the two sides of the canyon, but much of it had collapsed. Chunks of wooden railing were missing, and moss grew everywhere.

"It's like a bridge to nowhere," I said, looking down at the surging river. A canoe on the bank looked small from that height. I began to feel nervous.

"Look," Dawn said, "There's a couple of cabins. Let's take a look."

We followed a path along the lip of the canyon toward the closest cabin. An enclosed porch was cluttered with discarded work clothes, a rusty axe, a scythe and cartons of old beer bottles.

The cabin had just one room. A mirror hung near a bed where I saw a jumbled sleeping bag. There were a couple of chairs, a table and a big stove with a box of firewood beside it.

"At least this place is cozy," I said, walking over to warm my hands at the stove. "Is that rain I hear?"

Dawn glanced up at the roof, then looked at the fat drops splattering against the window. "I don't think it'll last. Let's wait it out in here."

"Okay, I guess that's . . . wait a minute!"

"What?"

"We came out here looking for Dark-Sky Thunder, right? I figured he'd be living in a tent, but what if he's using a cabin instead?"

Dawn looked at the sleeping bag on the bed. At the

same moment I stared at the warm stove.

We looked at each other. Then I raised my eyes to the mirror, where the door was reflected. It was slowly opening.

11

Dark-Sky Thunder stepped into the cabin. "What are you doing here?" The man's big body filled the doorway. His face was angry. My hands started to shake, but Dawn just looked at him defiantly.

"We've come about the mask."

"You've got it with you?" Dark-Sky Thunder glanced around the cabin. "Where is it?"

"Let's talk money first. How much are you willing to pay?"

"I'm not paying any more than was agreed."

"So," Dawn exclaimed. "You are involved with the mask. I knew it."

Dark-Sky Thunder stared at her, then turned to me. "What's this about?"

"I'm . . ."

Dawn grabbed my arm. "Don't say a word. We're getting out of here."

"Hold it." Dark-Sky Thunder raised his hand. "You're not going anywhere."

Dawn tried to push past the man, but he grabbed her with a big hand and shoved her to the floor. "You, too," he said to me. "On the floor." I moved closer to Dawn and sat down. I wasn't interested in being a hero now.

"Okay," he said, "where's the mask?"

Dawn shrugged. "I don't know."

"You're lying."

"I'm not! But I'd never tell you anyway. The mask belongs to my people."

He smiled. "It was kind of you to take the mask out of the museum for me. Until then I'd been beaten by the security."

"But you weren't Bear. You're too tall."

"That's right. I had someone working for me, and he wore the bear regalia. Then he was supposed to give me the mask, but everything got messed up."

"Why did you want it?"

"For money, of course. I was hired by someone to get the mask. I was promised a lot of cash if I was successful."

"Who hired you?"

Dark-Sky Thunder laughed. "Do I look dumb enough to answer that?"

"Your boss was going to sell the mask to a crooked dealer?"

"That's none of my business. And none of yours, either. What are you doing here? That's what I can't understand."

"Why should I tell you? You've caused nothing but trouble ever since you came to Hazelton. That's . . ."

Dawn paused, staring at the door. It squeaked on its hinges, then suddenly burst open. Standing there was Bear with the revolver. Aiming it straight at Dark-Sky Thunder, Bear forced the man back against the wall. Then he motioned at us to escape through the open door. Dawn jumped up, but I was such a nervous wreck that I couldn't move. As Bear reached down a hand to help me, Dark-Sky Thunder leapt forward and hit him hard on the side of his face. The mask went flying. The person wearing it was Ezra!

He staggered under the force of the blow, then somehow recovered and drove his shoulder into Dark-Sky Thunder's stomach. The pair fell to the floor and struggled desperately, but Dark-Sky Thunder was too strong for Ezra. He yelled in pain as his body was hammered against the wall, then gave up when Dark-Sky Thunder grabbed the gun and pointed it at him.

Dawn rushed to her brother. "Ezra, are you all right?"

"My ankle. It's twisted."

Dark-Sky Thunder waved the gun. "Get away from him."

"But he's hurt."

"Get away, and I mean that."

There was real menace in his voice. Dawn backed away from Ezra, then looked at him with a face that was deeply shocked. "Was it really you?"

Sweat was running down Ezra's face. He looked so sad leaning against the wall. "Yes," he said quietly. "I'm the one who stole the mask."

"But why?"

Dark-Sky Thunder laughed. "It was my plan. My boss wanted the raven mask but couldn't figure out a way to steal it from the museum. When we realized the security system at the museum was too strong, we decided to sucker Ezra into getting the mask out of the building for us."

Dawn looked at her brother. "You stole it for money?"

"Of course not," he said miserably. "But I stole it for pride, and maybe that's worse."

Dark-Sky Thunder smiled. "My boss has connections with international museums. We promised your brother some prestige exhibits if he got us the mask."

"I was desperate," Ezra said. "Museums kept turning me down. They kept saying I had to mature as an artist."

Dawn looked at her brother. "Why did you talk me into borrowing the mask from the museum?"

"That curator's soft on pretty faces. I knew he wouldn't give you an argument." There were tears in Ezra's eyes. "Please forgive me, Dawn. I shouldn't have used you like that."

"Of course I forgive you," Dawn said gently.

"Ezra," I asked, "why didn't you give Dark-Sky Thunder the mask the night you stole it?"

"Because things weren't like I expected. First of all, I didn't even get my hands on the mask until I'd followed you two home and taken it from the crawl space. Dark-Sky Thunder had driven to a party in Terrace to give himself an alibi, so I had some time to think. I had some doubts, so I hid the mask in the church tower until I decided what to do. When I saw how upset Dawn was, I was really confused."

"That's why you were so upset on our fishing trip?"

Ezra nodded. "I'd had a meeting with Dark-Sky Thunder and he was really angry. He wanted the mask badly—he even threatened to hurt you, Dawn. I didn't know what to do. I even thought of heading into the forest like Gun'an'noot."

"Oh, Ezra." Dawn squeezed his arm sympathetically.

"I finally decided to return the mask to the museum. I couldn't stand what was happening to you, and I felt so guilty. I love our people, and I realized how much I'd hurt everyone. I waited until after the death feast to slip into the church wearing my bear regalia in case I was spotted. When I heard noises outside, I hurried down to the sanctuary and hid. Then you found the mask in the tower, Dawn, and I thought all my problems were solved. I knew you'd give it back to the museum. But then I heard you talking about fingerprints and realized mine were all over the mask."

"So you stole it again."

Ezra nodded. "When I learned about the attack on you two in the gravehouse, I figured Dark-Sky Thunder was carrying out his threat. Right then I decided to give him the mask."

Dark-Sky Thunder laughed. "A simple scare works wonders. My boss thought I'd lost my touch when you wouldn't hand over the mask, but I came through."

Dawn looked at him. "So you're the person who phoned me."

"Yeah. I waited in Kispiox until I saw people leaving the death feast. When you got home I phoned, then headed for the cemetery. I could tell from your reaction on the phone that you'd go to the gravehouse."

"Then you locked us in."

Dark-Sky Thunder shrugged. "You were never in danger. I just tossed some pebbles on the gravehouse roof to scare you."

"But then you set the place on fire!"

He grinned. "That's what I wanted you to think, so you'd tell Ezra. I knew that would make him turn over the mask. But there was never a fire. I set off a smoke bomb outside the gravehouse, then removed the chunk of wood that I'd pushed against the door. You weren't in any danger."

Ezra shook his head unhappily. "I was so scared for you kids, I had to give Dark-Sky Thunder the mask. He'd got a message to me saying he was here and I drove out this morning with the mask. Then I heard you two coming, so I hid in the forest. When I saw Dark-Sky Thunder come back I knew there'd be trouble, so I grabbed the bear regalia from my car and ran back here."

"But Ezra," I said, "why did you need the regalia?"

"I hoped I could hide my identity from you and Dawn."

Dark-Sky Thunder looked at him. "Okay, let's get this over with. I need the mask now. My boss is arriving here soon, and I want to collect my money. Then I can finally get out of this dump."

Dawn looked at her brother. "Who's his boss?"

"I don't know."

Suddenly she whirled toward the door. *"Who's there?"*

Every eye flashed to the door. I saw a blur of motion as Dawn's hand went to the box beside the stove. In a single motion she grabbed a thick chunk of wood and brought it down on Dark-Sky Thunder's wrist. With a cry of pain he dropped the gun. Dawn sprang forward, seized the gun and aimed it at Dark-Sky Thunder.

"Kneel down!" When the man hesitated, she stepped closer. "I mean it."

Slowly he dropped to his knees.

"Ezra, can you walk?"

He tested his ankle, then shook his head. "No."

"Where's the mask?"

"In the back seat of my car."

"Is it safe there?"

"I don't think so. The car's unlocked, and Dark-Sky Thunder's boss is coming out here. My car's parked at the end of the dirt road. His boss will park there, too, and see the mask."

I looked at Dawn. "I'll go for it. You keep this guy covered."

She hesitated, then nodded. "Okay, Graham. Bring the mask back here, and we'll wait for the boss to show up."

Rain struck my face as I left the cabin. The path was slippery and I stumbled several times in my hurry to reach Ezra's car. Wet branches slapped my face, forcing me to take off my glasses as I ran. Although the world became a blur, I recognized the remains of the abandoned houses and the school. Then I found the path and followed it to the dirt road.

I turned down it and within minutes reached Ezra's car. Putting on my glasses, I opened the car door. On the back seat was the mask.

"At last! Have you ever caused a lot of trouble, Mr. Raven."

I slammed the door and stood on the road studying the mask. It seemed impossible that only a few days had passed since it was first stolen.

Then, as I stood on the road holding the mask, I slowly became aware of a car motor somewhere in the forest. Dark-Sky Thunder's boss! Turning toward the safety of the trees I started running, but my foot slipped on some mud and I fell.

My knee hit a rock, sending spasms of pain through my body. I crawled desperately toward the forest, hoping I could reach it before I was seen. But I wasn't fast enough. As I reached the trees I heard a car door slam and a voice call my name.

I crashed through the forest with the mask in my arms and finally reached the clearing beside the school. Pausing for a moment, I clutched the mask tightly and stared at the dark sky while one terrible thought ran through my mind.

I had recognized the voice of Dark-Sky Thunder's boss.

I had to either get back to the cabin where Dawn was waiting, or find my bike and ride to town with the mask. Either way I couldn't hang around the school forever.

The air was cold but the rain had stopped. I decided I had to warn Dawn, so I started along the path and soon reached the wrecked houses. Something moved behind one of the walls, then Virginia Lynch stepped into sight.

She didn't see me. With a frowning face she searched the clearing, then turned her eyes to the forest. As I stepped backwards I heard the loud *crack!* of a stick breaking under my foot.

"I see you, Graham," Virginia called. "I know you've got the mask."

Turning, I took off down the path. I raced through the forest, trying to avoid the wet branches, then reached the clearing where I could see the ruined bridge and the distant cabin where Dawn was waiting.

I could hear Virginia gaining as I tried desperately to reach the cabin. But I knew I couldn't make it, so I swerved sideways onto the bridge. It swayed under my weight as I ran along the warped timbers to the place where they ended, high above the river.

I turned and looked at Virginia. She stood at the end of the bridge, staring at me. "Why did you run out there, Graham?"

"Stay away. You're not getting the mask."

"Don't be a silly boy. Give it to me."

I shook my head. "Come closer and I'll drop the mask into the river. It will be lost forever."

Virginia smiled. "You don't mean that."

"Oh, yeah? Just watch me."

She walked onto the bridge. "Give it to me."

"Here it goes," I yelled, swinging the mask into the air.

"Don't!" Virginia stopped dead. "That mask is priceless."

"Is that why you hired Dark-Sky Thunder to steal it? Just so you could make some money?"

She shook her head. "It's not like that at all, Graham. You just don't understand. There's a collector who has some outstanding masks. All he needs is one from the Gitksan and he'll have the most perfect collection in the world. Can you deny him that, when the Natives have so many? So give me the mask and I'll be out of your life forever. You'd like that, wouldn't you, Graham?"

"I just remembered something. You said Dark-Sky Thunder was too tall to be Bear, but you weren't there when the mask was stolen. I should have realized you were involved."

"Better stick to movie-making as a career. You're not cut out for detective work."

"My dad's sure going to be hurt by all this."

"He'd never have known anything if you hadn't come snooping around here today. So it's your fault, not mine."

"How can you say that? You're the one who came to Hazelton to steal the mask. I bet you lied about being an anthropologist. You didn't know anything about the gravehouses and you're supposed to be an expert on the Gitksan."

"So what? I learned enough about them from your mother's books to fake my way through. I've done that in other parts of the world without any trouble."

"So you've stolen other masks. How's my dad going to feel when he finds out?"

"I'm sorry I've hurt him. I mean that. If I'd met a good person like your father just once in my life maybe I wouldn't be standing on this bridge arguing with you. But now I'm sick of talking. I want that mask, Graham, and I suspect you're too soft-hearted to throw it into the river. It's too important to Dawn."

"Get back," I warned.

"You're scared, aren't you?" Virginia moved toward me. "I heard what happened on the suspension bridge. Your father told me you're terrified of heights. Just give me the mask and I'll help you back."

Dropping to my knees, I put my hand on a support beam and swung over the side of the bridge. For a moment I dangled, then my feet connected with a cross-beam. As I began climbing down, I glimpsed the surprise on Virginia's face.

"Come back! You'll fall."

I tried to say something, then moaned when my boot slipped on a mossy beam. Closing my eyes, I reached cautiously down with my foot. It touched wood that seemed solid. I went lower, feeling the wind rushing against my face. From below came the roaring of the river through the canyon.

"Come back, Graham!"

My whole body was shaking. I wanted just to cling to the bridge and pray for rescue. Somehow I found the strength to move lower. Then I stopped again. The river was closer now, and Virginia's cries were harder to hear. Quickly I went lower, and then my feet touched rocky ground.

Looking up, I saw Virginia coming down the side of the bridge. At that moment I heard a cry and turned to see Dawn racing down a path that led from the cabin above. "This way, Graham," she called, pointing at a canoe near the water.

I stumbled across the rocks, then put the mask into the canoe. "Is Ezra okay?" I shouted as we hauled it toward the water.

"Yes. He's guarding Dark-Sky Thunder with the gun."

"How'd you know I was here?"

"I looked out the cabin window and saw you climbing down the bridge."

My feet splashed through the water as we got the

canoe away from shore. "Hurry up, Dawn!" I called as I climbed into the bow. "Virginia's right behind you."

The woman's face was ugly with anger as she came across the rocks. Dawn pushed the canoe farther from shore, then jumped into the stern and grabbed a paddle. As she drove us toward deeper water, Virginia reached the river. Pulling off her jacket, she waded in.

"She's coming after us!"

"Well, she can't catch us now."

"Where are we going?"

"This river runs all the way to Hagwilget and Hazelton."

"Have you been on it before?"

"No."

Turning, I looked downstream. "What's that?" Spray billowed into the air and I could hear a roaring that rapidly grew louder. We were travelling swiftly, borne along on the green water as the canyon walls closed in on both sides. The river surged against them, leaping into the air in foaming waves.

"Rapids!" I screamed. "Straight ahead!"

Cold spray stung my face. The noise was terrible. Waves raced in all directions as we plunged down between huge boulders, rolling and twisting. The canoe leapt into the air, then smashed down against the surging water. From the corner of my eye I saw Dawn battling the river with her paddle. Over and over her skill saved us from crashing into the rocks, and then suddenly it was over. The canoe slipped through a final patch of foaming white water and was safe.

"We did it!" I turned around to grin at Dawn but my movement was too sudden. With a sickening motion the canoe rolled over and freezing water buried me. As my lungs screamed, my body smashed against rocks and then hands grabbed my hair. Within moments I was dragged above the surface. As I spluttered and coughed Dawn's hands pulled me through the roaring water toward shore.

As my feet hit a rock, I was released. I thrashed around in the water, then managed to stand. Beside me was Dawn, soaking wet but grinning. "You did it, Graham!"

"Did what?" I asked through chattering teeth.

She pointed at my hands. For the first time I realized I was still holding the mask. As I stared at it Dawn stepped closer and gave me a kiss that I'll remember until I'm old and grey.

"My hero," she said, smiling.

"You've just given me an idea for a wonderful ending to my film," I said, grinning.

"Want to rehearse again?"

"You bet."

12

In Hagwilget, we called the police in time for them to set up a roadblock and catch Virginia as she tried to escape. The Mounties then picked up Dark-Sky Thunder and Ezra, who were both charged with the theft of the mask. But Dawn's parents found out that Ezra might only get probation because he'd been threatened when he was going to return the mask. The police were also impressed that after Dark-Sky Thunder gave him the gun, Ezra had emptied it of bullets so there'd never been a danger of anyone being shot.

Although Dawn's parents were still worried about Ezra, they decided to celebrate the mask's safe return with a small get-together, so people gathered in their yard one evening to enjoy barbequed salmon and other traditional Native foods. I stood by the cooking pit, feeling my mouth water as I watched sockeye salmon being cooked over red-hot embers.

"What are those things?" I whispered to Dawn, looking at a plate heaped with little black objects.

"Oolichans." When I looked blank she smiled. "They're fish. My people used them as candles in the old days."

"Really?"

"Oolichans are so greasy they'll actually burn after being dried. But nowadays we either eat them or boil them for their oil."

"What do they taste like?"

She gestured at the plate. "Try one."

I picked up an oolichan. It stared at me with vacant eyes. Two rows of little teeth gleamed in its open mouth. "Am I supposed to eat the head, too?"

She grinned. "That's right."

I glanced around the yard. Most of the guests were chatting with each other, but I noticed a few people watching me. Taking a deep breath, I put the fish in my mouth. As I bit off the head there was a crunching sound that almost made me gag. Then I chewed and swallowed as quickly as I could, trying not to think about those empty eyes and the rows of little teeth.

"Not bad," I said, coughing.

"Wash it down with some *yal'is*."

"I've heard of that stuff. What is it?"

"Whipped soapberries."

Dawn went into her house and returned a few minutes later with a crystal glass filled with a white froth that looked delicious. I helped myself hungrily to a heaping spoonful and then felt my taste buds explode.

"Yech! It tastes like soap."

She laughed. "That's where the name comes from." Taking the glass from me she quickly ate it all, then wiped her mouth. "Wonderful. It takes a while to get used to our food but try the salmon. I know you'll like that."

"Sounds good."

When my plate was heaped high I found a garden chair and sat down to eat. All of the dancers had come to the party, along with some other kids from our school, and it was good to see them laughing together with Dawn. A lot of them had already congratulated me on helping to recover the mask, so I was feeling pretty good. Even my dad was at the party, and I saw him smiling for the first time since he'd learned the truth about Virginia.

Then I heard the roar of a motorcycle and saw Connor Gentry arrive in a cloud of dust. When he came into the yard he saw Dawn beside me and walked over.

"I guess I gave you a rough time after the mask was stolen," he told Dawn. "I've come to apologize."

"That's okay, Connor. Now come and get some food. You're way too thin."

I felt a stab of jealousy as she took his arm and they walked together to the table. But then Connor surprised me by leaving Dawn and crossing the yard with his plate to sit beside me.

"Congratulations, Graham. I heard about your heroics at the ghost town."

"Thanks."

As I swallowed some salmon I studied his face and

decided he must have been born with that sour expression. I watched him eating potatoes covered with oolichan oil. Then I put down my plate.

"Would you answer a question for me?"

"Sure."

"Did you hide something in a stove at the rodeo grounds?"

He looked at me in surprise. "How did you know that?"

"Well . . . um. . ."

"Okay, I won't ask. Actually, I use that old stove to hide my fishing gear because I'm out at the Kispiox River a lot, and there's no sense in hauling everything back and forth on my motorcycle. Last week I decided to fish the Skeena, so I went to the rodeo grounds to get my gear."

I nodded. "That's when I saw you. To tell the truth, I thought you'd hidden the mask in the stove."

"So you thought I was the thief. Why didn't you phone the police?"

"Ezra said not to. Obviously that's because he knew you weren't guilty. Besides, Dawn couldn't believe you were involved."

"That's nice to know. Believe it or not, I suspected Dark-Sky Thunder was bad news from the moment I met him. He asked if he could pitch his tent in my field, then asked me a bunch of questions about 'Ksan."

"Like what?"

"Where the masks were kept, what kind of security the museum had, that kind of thing. After the robbery I was sure he was involved, but I couldn't prove anything and neither could the Mounties. His alibi for the evening was iron-clad. So I began hanging out with the guy, hoping I could somehow trick him into admitting he was involved in the theft. Finally he got angry and accused me of treating him like some kind of low-life, so I kicked him off my land. I figured the mask was lost forever after that, but you and Dawn came through for us all."

Connor returned to the table for more food. Then I saw the Einsteins approaching.

"Have you got a minute, Graham?"

"Sure."

Pa Einstein held up a video cassette. "Know what this is?"

My body turned cold. "I bet that shows me falling into the slime pit. Are you going to show it here?"

"Graham," Ma Einstein said, "everyone in Hazelton knows what happened at the ghost town. We've heard how you climbed down the bridge with the mask, despite your fear of heights, and then kept it safe when the canoe capsized."

"You and Dawn were very brave," her husband said. "We want to say thanks."

"That's nice of you, but . . ."

"And there's a special way we can show our appreciation."

Going to the fire, he dropped the video cassette into the glowing embers. The plastic smouldered, then began to warp in the heat. As I stared at it, Pa Einstein gave my arm a friendly squeeze.

"Your mother would be proud of you, Graham. You've got her strength of character."

I watched them walk away, then I thanked Dawn's

parents for the party. A short while later I'd collected some wood and tools from the vicarage and, with King at my side, was climbing the path to the graveyard.

When I reached it, I looked at the town spread out below. Through my hands I framed the sun as it dropped toward the mountains, turning the river to gold. In the past few days I'd lost interest in using Hazelton for a horror film. Instead I'd begun writing a script built around the legend of Simon Gun'an'noot. It would tell about his adventures in the wilderness, and the legends of the Gitksan.

At last I walked to Mom's grave and stood looking at it. Ever since the death feast I'd been thinking about what the Gitksan did when they lost someone they loved. I couldn't carve a totem pole to honour my mother but, like them, I could build a fence around her grave. It was maybe a small thing, but it was important to me.

So I began work on a fence. As I did, I felt really good.

About the Author

BRENDA SILSBE

This photo of Eric Wilson was taken in northern British Columbia while he researched this story. He became friendly with many people including the Gitksan, whose name means "People of the River of Mists." With them he enjoyed such adventures as a trip down the rapids of the Bulkley River and discovering the unique taste of soapberries and oolichans! Although Eric describes real places like 'Ksan in this mystery, the story itself and all the characters come only from his imagination.

VANCOUVER NIGHTMARE

A Tom Austen Mystery

ERIC WILSON

Tom tried to go lower but his foot slipped and dropped into open air. An electric shock of fear passed through him . . .

A chance meeting with a drug dealer named Spider takes Tom Austen into the grim streets of Vancouver's Skid Road, where he poses as a runaway while searching for information to help the police smash a gang that is hooking young kids on drugs.

Suddenly unmasked as a police agent, Tom is trapped in Vancouver's nightmarish underworld as the gang closes in, determined to get rid of the young meddler at any cost.

"Tom Austen has so much love and caring inside him."
—*Tara W., Pointe Claire, Québec*

DISNEYLAND HOSTAGE

A Liz Austen Mystery

ERIC WILSON

The air was blasted by the huge rotors of a helicopter which roared in above the wall and hovered over the fort, shaking us with the force of the wind storm it created.

On her own during a California holiday, Liz Austen is plunged into the middle of an international plot when a boy named Ramón disappears from his room at the Disneyland Hotel. Has Ramón been taken hostage? Before Liz can answer that question, her own safety is threatened when terrorists strike at the most unlikely target: Disneyland itself.

"When I was reading *Disneyland Hostage* I forgot that a man wrote it. Eric Wilson really knows what girls think."
—*Melissa F., Trail, British Columbia*

MURDER ON
THE CANADIAN

A Tom Austen Mystery

ERIC WILSON

The porter stood in the doorway of the sleeping car, waving his arm. "Come on, man!" he yelled. "Move those feet!"

The agonizing sound of a woman's scream hurls Tom Austen into the middle of a murder plot on board the sleek passenger train *The Canadian*. Who is responsible for the death of lovely Catherine Saks? As Tom investigates the strange collection of travellers who share Car 165, he gets closer and closer to the truth . . . and then, without warning, he is suddenly face-to-face with the killer, and his own life is threatened in the most alarming way possible.

"Suspenseful, humorous and full of action, it's the best book I've read."

—*Brauck W., Moose Jaw, Saskatchewan*

SUMMER OF DISCOVERY

ERIC WILSON

As his pulse raced, Ian sat staring at the piano—feeling terribly afraid and terribly excited.

Do ghosts of hymn-singing children haunt a cluster of abandoned buildings on the Saskatchewan prairie? The story of how the kids from Terry Fox Cabin answer that question will thrill you from page one of this exciting book. Eric Wilson, author of many fast-moving mysteries, presents here a tale of adventure, humour and the triumph of the human spirit.

"It was great! I liked how Ian slowly got over his fears and was ready to admit to them."
—*Matthew B., Winnipeg, Manitoba*

THE INUK MOUNTIE ADVENTURE

A Tom Austen Mystery

ERIC WILSON

Out on the frozen sea, they stopped to look at Gjoa Haven. The houses of the tiny hamlet seemed defenceless, huddled together under the roaring flames. Sam shook his head. "What a disaster for these good people."

What is the sinister conspiracy code-named CanSell, and how does it threaten Canada? Is the nation's handsome Prime Minister really what he seems? The truth is on a micro-cassette that Tom Austen must somehow find before a crucial vote by Canadians on the future of the country.

While on a school trip to Gjoa Haven in the high Arctic, Tom unexpectedly learns the cassette might be closer than he thought. Between drum dances and snowmobile chases across the tundra, Tom searches for the cassette and learns a valuable lesson from the Inuit about the futility of violence.

"I totally freak out when I find an Eric Wilson book I haven't read yet."

—*Danica J., Yellowknife, NWT*

"This story was full of action and suspense. I thought it written well and with good taste."

—*Ian K., Toronto, Ontario*